COMPANION PLANTS

Kathryn Roberts

Fomite
Burlington, VT

ISBN-13: 978-1-937677-79-4
Library of Congress Control Number: 2014950163

Fomite
58 Peru Street
Burlington, VT 05401
www.fomitepress.com

Cover Photo by Kathryn Roberts

For Adam

COMPANION PLANTS

I

THE FIRST TIME I MISSED MY PERIOD I washed a sprig of fresh parsley and pushed it as far into my vagina as I could reach. Every six hours, I boiled water and infused it with bunches of the fresh herb; after twenty minutes I gulped five tablespoons of the elixir with a vitamin C chaser. I switched out the sprig every twelve hours and didn't worry when some of the leaves, softened from hours stewing, tore off inside me and stayed lodged. The website said this was harmless and the bleeding would start within three days.

I wouldn't be able to hide a protruding stomach or a baby. Miscarriage sounded less deadly than abortion. Danny drove me to the natural foods store to buy organic parsley so I wouldn't risk injecting my body with pesticides when I pushed the stems inside. I spent the weekend moving from my bedroom to the bathroom and back, checking for blood. We never told Jackie.

The fear passed in thirty-seven hours after I finally bled, but I wondered if the parsley would work a second time if I got pregnant again. My mother refused to consider birth control for me—to her, the Pill was an excuse to have sex, and

I knew better than to ask. She read my journal weekly but thought I didn't know. So I detailed my days at school and headlined each page with a random verse from the devotional Bible that I never otherwise opened.

MY MOTHER DISCOVERED GOD after she discovered my father wrapped up in his secretary's fishnetted legs. At two years old I babbled out my laugher as he last kissed the top of my head and told me to be good. For years he was a presence relegated to birthday cards with a crisp one hundred dollar bill and a silver-plated framed photograph of him holding me above stalks of corn.

A month after my father left, Jackie and Danny's parents moved their family next door. My mother made zucchini muffins and packed them like raffia in a basket around tomatoes, cucumbers and string beans from our garden. She tied a ribbon to the handle and clutched me on her hip across the lawn with one arm, basket elbowed and swinging on the other, to greet the new neighbors. Our mothers became close friends within weeks, a result not from shared traits or a common sense of humor but from proximity. Soon, my mother car-seated me into the neighbors' station wagon every Sunday morning and we rode fifteen miles to the local Pentecostal church.

Jackie and Danny twins, I an honorary triplet to the two, we tantrummed, pranked, outgrew Sunday School teachers together. Sugar-voiced ladies asked our parents to pull us out of the children's classes and we were forced to sit in the sanctuary, hard-pewed and separated by adults. As teenagers required to attend youth group, we snickered across the room during devotions and at the altar when someone wailed or spoke in tongues, laughing without sound in the eye-language we knew from years of growing as a trio. Despite our defiance, constant exposure to strict parents and the fear-laden twice weekly lessons imprinted us. As much as we joked, we believed. We didn't know ideas that weren't infused with religion.

Our parents put us in a private Christian school. We sat, uniformed in skirts and dress pants, and learned history through a Bible-tinted lens. Science class avoided evolution, touching on the subject only to say atheists wanted to debunk the truth of creation but had no proof. When a student disagreed, it was considered back talk, and he was sent to the principal's office. Our literature was excerpted from major works, edited into story collections that dealt only with the superficial struggle between good and evil. Every Wednesday, the entire school assembled in the gym for chapel. Every afternoon, we studied God in Bible class. Girls and boys had to sit at least six inches apart and all the teachers carried rulers. Discussions weren't two-sided, but dictations, and we were drilled with an unspoken mantra of *don't question, don't refute.* Taught to absorb, believe, and be grateful we were introduced to our Savior early. Be grateful we missed the heartache of life without Him.

Danny trusted his teachers for years. Even as Jackie and I began to disentangle ourselves from commandments and sneak books to corners of the public library to learn what we were missing at school, Danny defended his lessons, echoed the rhetoric our teachers fed us daily. We dated for four months before Danny tongued into my mouth, another two before he slipped his hands up my shirt. He apologized afterward and avoided me for a week.

Danny began to doubt his upbringing after we caused the miscarriage. He angered through classes, picking fights with instructors. He bindered pages of handwritten notes he took while reading philosophy books and watching nature shows, lugged the evidence to each lecture and dared teachers to debate science. Given detention nearly every day, he used the time to write essays refuting religion. But he carried a pocket Bible hidden in his jacket and I saw him, closed eyes and head slumped down, lips mumbling inaudibly, sitting on moss at the edge of the small grove of trees that bordered his house.

Jackie relinquished the last of her faith two days before their eighteenth birthday, when Danny wrapped an old rope around the railing surrounding the second platform of their tree fort, tied the end around one of the bars they had held in place while their father drove nails through the scrap wood. Twenty feet above the ground, he climbed onto the railing, a loop fastened around his neck. When Jackie found him, he wasn't swinging like the corpses in films: head slightly tilted, peaceful closed eyes. His neck broke from the impact and his head leaned too far back, bruises painting his throat oceanic. His green eyes stared bloodshot at branches. There was no wind and he remained still as he had when they'd hidden in closets during hide-and-seek. Jackie sat cross-legged, crunched down leaves and dirt, threw acorns at Danny's corpse. I sat behind her when I arrived, folded my feet under her legs and she leaned back.

"But he got a haircut yesterday," she said.

Doubt sidled to me in adolescence as forbidden love: a cousin whose family refused to attend her commitment ceremony, a classmate taunted for kissing another boy. Now, years later, when my body, laid out and contorted before men, remains detached, my mind travels to a pond, Jackie lying on her back in a bikini of blue lines shot like electricity across a white background, dark tan arms folded behind her head on the raft. Loons break through the water and dive again, teaching the adolescents how to hunt, stitching a line of spotted black feathers across the lake. I climb out of the water, fish-belly my way onto the wooden float and lay my head on Jackie's ribcage. Every time a man comes inside me I am kissing Jackie, when he shoves my head down I am holding her hand. The summer ends with orgasm and I am back in the car, the hotel, my cheap studio apartment.

I imagine Jackie waking Danny in the womb, whispering *It's time*, voice soft but throaty already. He grabs her ankle, the kick their mother feels, Danny throwing himself around Jackie to stop her. *I'll go first*, she tells him. *Follow me when you're ready.*

Twins share history; fraternal not DNA-replicated, but carried in, wrestled with mother's body together. Growing up a single person, parents referring to them as *the twins*, not Jackie and Danny. They shared bunk beds, switching off top and bottom every six months, until at twelve their parents enforced separate rooms. Late at night, Danny crossed the Jack and Jill bathroom to Jackie's room, joining our sleepovers.

Our houses were close enough to walk across the lawns in two minutes. The next nearest neighbor was too far away to see. Every summer night our families barbecued on concrete patios. My mother *tsk*ed at their mother when she suggested setting her up with a single man from the church; their father charred burgers and hot dogs but smothered them with ketchup so we couldn't tell. We made individual forts and exchanged old corn cobs like currency, buying access to each others' secret lairs where we cooked meals of husks and rotten tomatoes. At night, we climbed up on the roof with Jackie and Danny's dad and watched the lightning bugs Morse code the fields.

Danny captivated me, his shied away, down-turned manner begging me to decipher him. In sixth grade, Jackie black-eyed an eighth grader during recess when he laughed at her brother's awkward basketball shots. But at home, she followed Danny around and mimicked his habits: mismatched socks, potato chips on chocolate ice cream, bed moated with books.

AFTER I FOUND JACKIE IN THE WOODS, she climbed to the second platform, untied the rope and dropped Danny to the ground. He splayed, neck oddly angled, one leg crumpled behind the other out front, but his hands folded across his chest. Jackie jumped to earth, pulled apart his hands, unbuttoned his cobalt Oxford shirt and dragged it off his body. When she ripped off her sweater and sleeved her arms in his shirt, she couldn't close the buttons. She wore it anyway, trying to absorb Danny, morph into him as I held her, shift inside to create space for him. The greatest tribute she could give him was assuming his life, consuming his presence as if pumping his heart, breathing his lungs.

We held hands at his funeral, three days after Jackie tried to convince her parents to cremate Danny. If she had run to them right away, called them, crying, from the small grove of trees behind their house—*Help!*—maybe they would still hear her. But after they found us sitting together in a pile of leaves at the base of the tree, staring, Danny mangled and shirtless, their daughter dressed in their son's shirt, her parents stopped listening. My mother only let me near Jackie because she hoped neither of us would hurt ourselves with the other around.

The headstone read *Daniel* and I pretended he wasn't beneath it, that his parents had given in and Jackie had scattered Danny across the cornfields where we used to run long afternoons, lost in the aisles that rowed our childhoods into infinite neat lines. We spent our first years believing our lives would unfold across the farms, connected by the god who judged us and the families that guided us to Him. When we found our way out of the corn maze we spent the first few seconds disoriented and unsure if we'd arrived at the same house where we'd begun. Jackie and I outgrew the days between the stalks before Danny, and he begged us to run across our roots with him again.

Jackie crawled into my arm, shouldered her head to me. My eyes focused on the periphery. A sky stretched with thin clouds, Jackie's unbuttoned charcoal peacoat over Danny's forest green sweater, black patent leather Mary Janes on a white-tighted toddler, a woman's chipped French-tipped fingernails. The pastor spoke of forgiveness as members from our church avoided each other's eyes. No one mentioned suicide. The lowered coffin signaled finality and even in the expressions of sympathy, no one offered the usual solace *At least he's with our Lord*. Most people left the post-burial reception after a quick pass around the living room. Our mothers walked upstairs after only ten minutes and Jackie's father followed soon after. Jackie fell asleep in a chair, staring at the untouched snacks on the plate sitting on her lap.

AT MIDNIGHT I WHISPERED OUT OF THE HOUSE and returned to the grave. I dug my fingers in the soil, wanting the dirt under my nails, leaving my hands half-buried for too long. Parsley ends life but also begins, and I covered the length of Danny with seedlings. Every year when it blooms the wasps

will come and patrol the cemetery, protect the flowers growing from neighboring bodies; swallowtail butterflies will lay
larvae in the leaves and yellow-dotted black and green stripes
will caterpillar up and down the plants, feeding, until they
transform and take flight. I imagine Danny offering up himself to the roots. His fingers reach to draw the plants to him
and as he ages he will give birth to offshoots. His parents will
mourn the meaningless loss of their son while his body makes
sense of a life in the garden, his tribute that erupts in fragrant
leaves spreading from his chest across the graveyard and into
the endless plains.

ONTHS AFTER THE FUNERAL, we drove away from the Quad Cities in Jackie's car. Our parents thought we were going to a graduation party but we reached our classmate's house and kept going west, my backpack in the backseat and her trunk packed full of clothes, water, trail mix, and a small cooler of food. Jackie brought Danny's old 35-mm Pentax SLR, insisting we record the trip on something tangible, negatives to back up. *Adventure looks better later when you can't preview the images*, she insisted. *No room for self-editing as you go.*

Through images we discovered ourselves, defined our edges in photograph-captured outlines. Even a mirror or window shifts around your boundaries. But in photographs the edges stick to glossy paper, engrave images that cannot shift: memories of Jackie thin and thinner, shoulder blades protruding like over-sized chicken wings and jeans that slid off her hips even when belted. She fell asleep after an autumn funeral and awoke without hunger.

At every rest stop Jackie grabbed the camera, shot frames, shielded it from the sun as she switched out the film. When I took cell phone snapshots as we drove, she screeched to the side of the highway and refused to start again until I promised to keep the phone shut off. Iowa stretched out as familiar—school trips across the state, county fairs, summer camps. The terrain shifted imperceptibly as we left the state, but Jackie stopped by the Welcome to Nebraska sign for a photograph anyway. She had never been west of Iowa.

When I found out I was pregnant, Danny sat on the side of our high school soccer field with me as night edged in and begged me to leave with him.

"I have a cousin in California. We can keep the baby," he said.

Silence aches because it is unanswered but definitive. I lay on my back, pinprick holes punching through the sky, first just one, then faster as dusk slid away. Danny ran his fingers across my scalp, at first gentle, soon hair-pulling. I reached to sleeve his cheek, tears in fabric so they wouldn't leave traces on the ground. I couldn't stand the thought of physical remnants.

"This can't have happened, Danny. I don't want to remember."

We never told Jackie. Stories become memory when passed to others, in the retelling we make it real.

We reached the outskirts of Cheyenne in time to watch the sun rise in the barren landscape, to shutter-click a memory of presence. The lonely plains stretch across acres, define the earth with monotony, but the Wyoming isolation stunned us. Mountains, sparse plants across dust, a single road interrupting. Layers of color in the sky dotted with the bug-splatter spots on the windshield. Pink ground, pink hills, pink road.

Jackie pulled into a rest area and made me a breakfast of dried mango, vanilla Greek yogurt, and stale grocery store croissants. She watched my hands move to my mouth, then stared across the hills to our side. The rocks jetting through pink earth fed her. When her stomach voiced loud enough for me to hear, she denied pain.

"I no longer feel anything," she said.

I spoon-fed her two bites of yogurt before she doubled over and threatened to throw up.

IN THE FAMILY RESTROOMS, the only individual door-locked spaces in a country releasing itself to us in dusty yellow-lighted rest stops, we rinsed our hair in the sink and washclothed our bodies. Jackie's body was familiar, years of sleepovers and locker rooms together. But when I glanced at the mirror-girl standing beside me, bending to pull on dark-rinse skinny jeans, she was gone. In her place stood the wire framework for a bendable doll, begging to be covered in padding. Her skin hung on the wire, waiting to be filled, or to decay. I stared at her, disgusted, oddly allured, wondering at this transformation from living to halfway and trying to remember when it began. She moved her head and I looked back to the mirror, examined my cheekbones that hadn't shown sharp since middle school and wondered how much she weighed now.

"C'mon, love," she said. "We're almost to California."

At what point does mind relinquish power to body emaciated, inch so close to sluggish that it has no defense against an ache for food? Jackie swore she felt nothing, rumbling and sharp ache left behind in a grove of trees in Iowa. I imagined the pain of stomach grinding and gurgling against itself, acid dissolving only air. Her muscles adjusted soon after, agreeing to live on caffeine, killing off strands of themselves gradually. I wondered if her heart knew to hold onto itself, or if it gave willingly, too.

She tossed at night when we slept in the car, woke up and said her bones wouldn't let her rest. Lying down hurts as much as sitting hurts as much as standing. Where do you move when the ache won't stop? Disappear. Elevate mind to place beyond the dull throb of bones settling without cushion between. Denounce food and glorify restraint. She shivered in her sweater under blankets even when the air ran in the 80s. Her fingers, always cold.

WE LURCHED THROUGH UTAH, skirting Salt Lake City, passing over mountains. The car hesitated with each incline, slowing to forty even when the gas pedal rode on the floor. We hit the edge of the city, peaks rising to our left and the vast white ground spreading to our right, and pulled into a gas station. I'd begged Jackie to eat breakfast, but she refused and we'd ridden in silence for hours.

"I need an apple. Will you grab it and a diet pop while I run to the bathroom and meet me outside?" Jackie asked and tossed me a few bucks.

I sat crosslegged on the grass at the edge of the parking lot and listened to the seven voicemails my mother had left me before my mailbox ran out of space. Jackie insisted we not contact our parents, but I imagined my mother's tightening chest as she grabbed her old flip phone every fifteen minutes to check for the little message icon. While I was growing up, my mother had been the parent to call at every sleep over, the one to check my homework for errors each night before I packed it in my bag, the one to bundle me up when other kids were wearing tee-shirts. I imagine she feared me walking away one day and not coming home as my father had and webbed me to her with strands of worry.

I held my breath, ready to end the call, but she didn't pick up. She must be at church. Familiar beep, a few seconds paralyzed, finally,

"We're okay. Decided to take a trip. Not sure when I'll be home." At the last second, I added, "Love you."

When I was seven, I read a novel about a girl whose father died before she could apologize for an argument that ended with *I hate you*. Now, I couldn't finish a conversation with my mother without a compulsory affection; my mind focused on the unspoken words obsessively until I blurted them out.

"Who were you talking to?" Jackie asked. "You didn't call home, did you?!"

"Yeah, but I just left a message saying we didn't know when we'd get back. Didn't say where we were."

"We were supposed to disappear."

I passed her the apple, soda and a small bag of trail mix. She shook her head at the dried fruit and nuts.

"You've got to eat more. Just take it in the car, okay?"

Jackie grabbed the plastic snack tube and set it beside her on the pavement. I knew she would leave it when we stood up, a present for some kid who only had enough quarters to pay for a pop. We stared silently at the mountains.

I wondered what it would be like growing up where the ground is uneven, where you wake up peaked-in. Snow-capped, cereal-bowled into a valley. After a lifetime spent running across flat earth, I imagined the mountains define you and the plains seem an oddity to someone from Salt Lake as much as the peaks unsettled me.

"You know Danny loved you, right?" Jackie said, still refusing to look at me.

She hadn't spoken his name in months. We'd never discussed the year I'd spent dating her brother, the months of circumventing our strict parents with a series of fabricated group dates. I looked at her, but she stayed profiled. My mind turned circles on itself. Did he talk about me with her or did she just suppose?

"We were sixteen..." I didn't know how to respond. I wanted to say what she needed.

"I didn't mean anything by it. Just wanted you to know in case he never told you. He never said anything, but I could tell. I was jealous of you two. Mostly of him."

Jackie slipped her hand into mine without looking over. We sat for several minutes, not speaking. I absorbed her through her bony fingers, drew the cold out of her skin, let my hand take on her smell. Clasped her fingers tighter and wiped my eyes across my shoulder. She turned, smiled, kissed my cheek, and stood.

"C'mon, let's get going."

She chased me across the parking lot, laughing. As we ran I worried, if she fell, would I be able to catch her in time or would she hit the asphalt and barely make a sound as she shattered into a thousand pieces of bone?

R EST STOP IN NEVADA. The sun fell over the desert hours before we decided to pull over. I quit asking to pause for snacks; when I looked at Jackie, I felt too guilty to eat. We piled out of the car, stretched, settled back in.

"Let's skip this stop and find a town," Jackie suggested. "We can get something to drink and camp out in a mall lot or something."

I nodded, "Definitely."

We'd spent the night before half-sleeping, parked in the brightest lit, still dim, spot in an isolated rest stop. We chose a place with lots of truckers camping so someone would hear us if we screamed. Though an individual trucker may seem dangerous, we wanted to believe that, as a lot, they'd be honorable. We needed to believe it. A mall or grocery store lot may be no better than a rest stop, perhaps, but neon signs and 24-hour gas stations blazed and flashed false comfort.

We pulled off the highway on a random exit. Megaplex gas station, deli, restaurant, mini-mart, arcade, and coffee shop. No mall or movie theater or other stores. One road leading back onto the highway, one disappearing into the dark. Inside, I lost Jackie. Forgot her for the aisles of granola bars and bags of chips. I grabbed two bottles of water and a Diet Pepsi, a sugary fake cappuccino from the instant machine, two hard-boiled eggs in a plastic cellophane-wrapped tray, and a triple-serving bag of white cheddar popcorn. Jackie stood just out of earshot behind me as I paid, but pieces of her voice reached me in waves.

"Sure…at the car…whatever's good."

She sidled to me and we hook-armed it outside.

"What's going on, Jackie?"

"Got us some beer. That guy's gonna bring it to the car," she nodded over her shoulder.

I'D HAD MY FIRST BEER TWO DAYS AFTER THE FUNERAL. Jackie and I sat on the edge of the same field where I refused Danny's offer to head west. After her brother died, the few times when Jackie's parents spoke, they whispered over her, as though she'd evaporated with her twin and speaking too loudly would rustle up memories. Her mother left three weeks later. When Jackie answered the phone the next afternoon, her mother paused, startled by the sound of a female voice.

"Tell John I've gone to live with my sister."

After that, she sent a letter once a month. No one opened them. Her husband never begged her home. If Jackie missed her mother, mourned or loathed her leaving, she hid it some-

20

where in her room, a field, the tree fort. In a house that rarely saw alcohol, there were suddenly bottles of beer every night, sometimes whiskey. Jackie snuck out a few rounds from the refrigerator and bicycled them in a basket to our spot. We worshipped our breath in the air, huddled under a blanket and yelled our stories of Danny into the night. The bike wobbled along with us on the way back and we slept until two the next day; we repeated the ritual every Saturday until too-deep snow covered the field.

JACKIE UNLOCKED THE CAR when she saw the guy approaching with a paper bag. He climbed into the back, shoved aside bags of empty pop bottles and stretched out his legs across the seat. His dusty hiking boot hooked my shoulder as he swayed his foot in rhythm to the electronica we played. Despite his mountain-man beard I figured he was in his early twenties. I fidgeted with the seat belt, turned so my left fingers grazed the door handle.

"Hey, I'm Luke." He stretched out his plaid long-sleeved arm and passed us each a Fat Tire. His eyes were a color that wavered between henna and mahogany, unusual but dull next to Jackie's bright green. He leaned back against the door, propped up his head on folded arms. This guy is harmless, I thought.

"So where are you headed?" Luke asked.

"We were thinking California," said Jackie, shrugging at me.

"For how long?"

Jackie and I stared at each other. We'd driven west only

knowing we wouldn't return until we were ready. The logistics of the trip—money, food, housing—we figured would show up. One morning we'd wake up and head home or find jobs.

"No idea," I said. "We've got no plans."

"Dude, you two should come up to northern Cali." Luke sloshed beer on his cargo pants as he hoisted himself into lean-forward position. "I'm riding up with friends, we've got work up there for the summer and fall. It's outdoor season, everyone needs extra help. Show up with us and you'll be all set."

"Outdoor season? Work doing what?" Jackie asked.

"Seriously? Helping with the plants, trimming in the fall." Luke laughed at our expressions. "You do know what Humboldt's famous for, right?" We shook our heads and he smiled. "Weed."

We drank another round of beer as we learned the details of our new jobs, a way to stay west-coasted for an entire season. Back home, any mention of marijuana on television made parents stammer and speak too loudly about random topics until they could hit mute or switch the station, shaking their heads. The only time I'd seen pot was in an upperclassman's old issue of *High Times* that he brought home from when he visited his brother at college.

When we finished the first six-pack, Luke bought another and we joined his friends in the old conversion van they were driving north. Jackie hit bottle four and slurred herself onto the lap of a lanky, blond-haired guy who'd introduced himself as Dustin. He laughed and kissed her neck.

22

I thought about grabbing her waist and leading her back to our car, protecting her. But from what? Our purpose was escape. Break what we know into as many pieces as we can, shake. Subtract, add, reassemble and set ourselves in a new world. *At least when she drinks she consumes something*, I thought.

We left our car in the parking lot. Eventually, Jackie's dad would wonder where she was. Before him, my mother would notify the police, even if I called to check in. We emptied the trunk, threw the keys inside, slammed the door down. Double-checked and empty, doors locked, the car waited, parked by the dumpster behind the gas station for someone to decide it was abandoned.

As we drove away—Jackie sleeping across the backseat of the van, her head in Dustin's lap, my head resting against the passenger's window, Luke's hand on my thigh—I wondered where the people in Nevada live. There were no houses visible from the highway cutting across the state. Only casino-town oases, series of hotels with pumped-in water and neon. Even the monstrous gas station, hubbed into the landscape by numerous truckers and vacationers trying to reach other states, seemed planted for travelers. As I fell asleep I imagined a desert filled with underground cave dwellers. Dark holes carved into the side of the earth, steps built down into subterrain. Walls drawn with elaborate manuscripts in pictures and words, narrating a life of shadows. Tunnels running between each home, through great halls, cafes and bathhouses, connecting an entire world. Beneath our wheels, people moved through the subways like alcohol through blood.

PHOTOGRAPHS CAN'T CAPTURE the first time seeing the desert. A childhood imagining of sand, dunes, maybe a cactus, resembles nothing of the expanse. The ground at the edge of the highway merges from asphalt to sand, which could be salt, mixed with dirt, stuccoed with sparse undergrown bushes. The land appears faked for scenic images, as though a studio dumptrucked in loads of earth and raked it flat in preparation for a film. It calls out for pulling over and touching. For running over the ground toward the hills where it morphs to bare rocks, climbs to flat crests and odd formations of orange stone.

We drove across the rest of Nevada in the afternoon, staring out the road-dusty windows at the foreign landscape. Luke drove at least twenty miles over the speed limit across the state. Every so often, he'd abruptly slam the brakes before heading around a bend or near an outcropping of rock, so when we'd pass the hidden cop car, we'd be going two miles under. He never failed to slow down in time. Dustin, Jackie, and Luke's other friends, Nick and Josh, sprawled unbuckled in the back of the van, asleep despite the sudden braking.

Someone had put on an old copy of *Back to the Future* on the built-in VCR television—"The movie was in the glovebox when we got the van," said Luke—and it played like a dated pop culture lullaby behind my head.

"Where are you from?" I asked Luke.

"Middle of nowhere, New Hampshire. You?"

"Iowa. Near the Quad Cities." When he shrugged, I didn't bother to explain. The four towns that meet at the edge of Iowa and Illinois were only names to him. The words hardly meant more to me. "Why'd you leave for California?"

"Eh, I was going to school in Boston but was bored out of my mind," said Luke. "My older brother took off and called me in October a couple years ago to tell me he'd dropped out and gone to California to help his friend with a business. My folks were pissed; I mean, they don't really care what he does if he's happy, but he was pulling a 3.8 at Dartmouth, starting center for the basketball team, a year away from graduation and they couldn't understand why he couldn't wait. He told me he was going to make money instead of paying for an education he didn't want."

"He didn't want? I mean, three years into Dartmouth?" My reaction was automatic, pre-programmed by years of my mother. "Why not just finish?"

"Have you ever done anything you wanted? I mean, something that your parents or teachers or friends didn't dictate?"

"Aside from this trip..." I stared out the window. My life had been goaled and gridded since before I was born. "Okay. So he went to Cali?"

Luke smiled. "It's alright, you know. I mean, you can't control everything."

"Anyway, your brother..."

"Yeah, well, he told me that he was bored with school and needed a change. That if he stayed at Dartmouth he'd end up with a job he hated, a wife for the sake of it, and a fast-track to a life of ordinary. I wanted to go out there right away, but he made me promise to finish up school first. I told him that was bullshit, that he quit so why couldn't I? He made me promise and told me I'd have a guaranteed income when I finished, which didn't seem too bad. But, by the time I hit senior year, I couldn't stand college anymore. My life was a series of regurgitations, I spit out exactly what my professors wanted and I got my As. Parents proud, all that. I called Bruce and told him I was coming early. That I understood why he quit and I'd be in Arcata in a couple weeks. I recruited Dustin, Nick and Josh, and here we are."

"Did you travel much? I mean, before this trip?"

"Yeah, backpacked across Europe after high school, spent some time in Peru. A semester abroad in South Africa. You?"

"Nope." I'd gone to Tennessee once, visited cousins and the Grand Ole Opry. My lack of experience embarrassed me. "Are you going to go back? I mean, to college?"

"Right now it seems pointless."

"And Bruce is okay with you dropping out?"

"He understood."

"Will he understand when you show up with a couple extra people?"

"Yeah, it'll be fine. People are a bit more relaxed out there. You don't need to worry so much. Just go with it."

I stared out the front window, watched the striations of sun and clouds, wondered if I would have seen the same land if I'd left years before. If Danny and I had fled in high school, told Jackie about the baby, pulled her with us, would Wyoming have overwhelmed us with pink, Nevada appeared such lonely orange? Would we have made it to the coast in a car our parents would have reported stolen or had the courage to ditch it and busk the rest of the way?

Courage arrived to me in pieces, segments of fear dissolving inside me, melting away with my memory of Danny. At sixteen I would have left but returned, too uncertain to dislodge from a mother who'd handed down phobias like heirlooms. Every denial of my anxiety was a rejection of her tradition. I wondered if this sudden letting go stemmed from growth or loss.

Luke kept smiling, even as he slammed on the brakes again. Jackie crawled forward and asked for water, clutching my armrest with her bony fingers like a nocturnal animal sluggish in the daylight. I watched the dusk take over the highway as we approached the California border. I tried to let go.

At the edge of California we passed through a booth, where we declared ourselves free of plants and animals. I wondered if the guards ever searched vehicles or if they just believed everyone at their word. My first glimpse of the state through the van's dim headlights, the lights that showed us only twenty feet ahead, was of the same road that passed through the desert, continuing through the customs security gate and disappearing ahead. The transition felt like crossing from Iowa to Nebraska. Changes in terrain happened in the center of the states, not the edges, and I wondered how you determine the heart of a state. How you decide if the landscape within means more to identity than the view of your outlines.

Dustin was driving now with Nick riding shotgun, the front windows rolled down, a pipe pulled out. The soft click of a lighter snapped through the car, the barely audible crackle, the ticking rasp of held in cough through nose. Josh, who earned his master's in philosophy from Tufts just before leaving the East Coast, debated Wittgenstein with Luke in the back seat. Jackie braided then unwound my hair, over and over again, as I rested my head on her lap. We listened to music on my phone—the *Straight Road Trippin'* playlist we'd created before leaving Iowa—the left earbud hooked into my ear, right nestled in hers. We'd driven for hours, but the guys wanted to push through, reach Bruce's place without stopping for the night. I felt like a child, wondering why we'd reached California but were still so far away from our destination. Could a state really be so large, so long, that five more hours of road curved before us?

CA-44 W becomes CA-299 W, twists itself through California, around ledges of rock that threaten to slide and only edged by thin guardrails, down snaked hills that promise to end only to climb again, through the Shasta-Trinity National Forest where trees rise up around you, tunnel the road like a closed-in race course, daring you to accelerate when you should slow. At night the landscape unfurls in sections, new slide frames with each sharp turn, each dissolution of fog in low-beams. The asphalt surface at the entrance to the forest is covered in splotches of red paint or earth that looks like blood across the road, an image remembered when animal warning signs flash yellow in peripheral vision.

Fifty miles to Arcata suggests, in number, an hour. In practice, two or more. As we climbed and descended, slithered around bends, Dustin too fast but controlled, I dozed to the rhythm of accelerate, brake, accelerate, brake. Fear grows from unknown boundaries, edges that drop abruptly and disappear into the dark, leaving no sense of distance. If you fall, for how long? Do you land after ten feet or crash to a ledge hundreds below? I found closed eyes easier than open with no focal point. Nick cursed the weather, insisting we'd have reached our destination already if it weren't for the fucking fog.

Slammed stop and Jackie's scream woke me. The rear of the van slid to the left as we gripped seats and Dustin worked the wheel, avoiding sliding across toward the sharp rock edge. A deer stood in the middle of the road, horns still small and new but body large enough to damage. He stood, staring at us, even as Dustin blared the horn. He finally spooked up the rocks to the right.

"Dude, if it hadn't been foggy..." Luke's voice trailed off.

The speed limit on the roads reaches forty, even around bends. Deer climb the cliffs as though they were flat, bound from the trees abruptly, disappear into the night. The only part of a deer that reflects light is the empty straight-on eyes.

BRUCE RAN OUT TO GREET US when we drove up. He resembled Luke only in the eyes, the same energetic brown stare. At least three inches shorter, head shaved, beardless and heftier, I would have guessed them distant cousins. But when he greeted us, he sounded so familiar that I thought he was lip-synching while Luke spoke.

"What's up, brah?" Bruce grabbed Luke and slapped his back. "Dude, Nick! Dustin! How the hell are you?!"

"Hey man, wasn't sure we'd make it! Almost crashed on the way up, it was epic," Dustin said as he pulled Jackie by the waist. "Bruce, Jackie. Jackie, Bruce. We picked these ladies up at a rest stop in Nevada."

"Yeah, man, is it cool if they crash here?" Luke asked. "Figured you could use some extra hands."

"Totally. No worries. Always nice to have someone show up with a couple pretty girls," Bruce winked in our direction. "C'mon in, guys. There's food if you're hungry. Plenty of beer in the fridge. Take whatever you want, let's chill for a bit, no?"

We semi-circled ourselves on the floor and on worn couches in the living room. Bruce wanted to know the details of the trip, Jackie and I added bits once the story hit Nevada. Dustin pulled out his pipe and Bruce passed him a jar with buds from his latest crop.

"Dude, smell that shit. New strain for this quarter. Smooth," he said. Dustin packed the bowl and passed the jar around. I deep-breathed the scents of earth, oregano, fruit, and dried lawn clippings and spun a dehydrated cone, crisp-leaved grayish green, in my fingers before handing off to Jackie. Luke whispered instructions in my ear when the pipe reached me, passing off the lean-in as affection. Thumb over hole, lighter click, breathe in, thumb off, breathe deeper. I held the smoke in my mouth, drew in a small breath, wisped it out after a few seconds. Luke passed me a beer when I started coughing. Someone grabbed a guitar, picked a soundtrack as we storied each other with our previous lives. We shared cigarettes on the lawn as rain frenzied over us.

As the sky inched pink, we set up tents in the backyard. Bruce had a closet full of camping equipment and gave us each a sleeping bag. Jackie and I shared a tent, zippered our two bags into one. She shivered herself next to me, propped my arm over her waist, nudged up my chin with her nose, and puzzled her head to my neck. I hooked my fingers in her sweatpants' waistband and we fell asleep.

WE WORKED MOST DAYS, learned to snip closely, quickly, carefully. Rub vegetable oil between fingers to rid of the residue. Sometimes everyone trimmed together, sometimes one or two joined others for jobs. Luke helped Bruce with the plants, Jackie and I helped other growers whose crops were already hung, dried, ready. Dustin, Nick and Josh wandered in and out. Everything relaxed, all the time. I sent my mother an e-mail to say I would be away indefinitely, then blocked her e-mail address from my inbox.

A week after we arrived, Jackie and I discovered the redwood forest at the edge of the city. We walked down a street and right into the grove, a path up from the road through old growth mulch. Jackie ran to a tree and tried to encircle it, her arms spanning less than a third of the visible arc. Lining either side of the path were broken sections of fallen trees, several-story stumps with tentacle roots twining around the forest.

Redwoods grow straight, trunks barely curved, branches' starting points too high to reach. Needles hundreds of feet above muddle the skylight and leave the floor in dusk all day long. Ferns stretch over the damp soil, a first-layer forest too thick to distinguish one plant from another. Moss eats its way up the trees and banana slugs ooze onto the muddy path.

We left the trail a few hundred yards into the woods, harbored ourselves into a trio cove of redwoods through a single-file sideways pass. I ran my fingers along the thick bark longitude lines that ridged up a tree. Jackie grabbed my waist, pulled me to cover her against a half-trunk, crawled her hands up my back, clenching the valley between my shoulder blades. She kissed under my chin as I foundationed my hands against the worn-smooth side of the stump. Her lips climbed toward mine. Short-breathed, wondering does kissing follow genders, do hands sliding set off nerves in different directions when the fingers are female. Only recently learned motions— *do I move in similar ways?*—but this felt like something making sense. My hips shifted second-natured and I bent down to meet her. We consumed each other, mouths trying to open wider than jaws. I'd never kissed like this. Yanked off shirts, lips traced lines across our bellies, wanting more but stopping, shy. Laughing, we pulled on clothes and tore through the ferns, tripping on piles of fallen needles and bark, rushing over a stream that barely runs.

Jackie grabbed my hand and wouldn't let go until we reached our campsite at Bruce's house. She swung herself in front of me to grab my other hand, back-stepping across the sidewalk, only to twist again to my other side and leave her arm across my waist. We talked about the salmon we were grilling for dinner, whether the guys would want to watch a film, if we should treat ourselves to new clothes.

I didn't have words for my mind fighting itself, arguing the thrill of Jackie against driven-in forbidden. But hands held through the streets and lips together felt as natural as lips against previous boyfriends, even more. Our first night back home, we let go of each other before dinner.

WE WERE STILL PATTERNING through the first weeks of a new infatuation, figuring out where we fell, together. We had no gauge for adult coupling, didn't know at what point during devouring each other *we* become *us.* Jackie called me her girl

34

friend, but I had been one to her since childhood and I struggled with the distinction between earlier and recent. Whenever we'd arrive back at camp, I'd shift out of her arm around my waist, retract my fingers from the base of her spine or the crevices of her hands.

"Why do you bother trying to hide it?" Luke asked me as Jackie walked into the kitchen and I picnic-tabled myself in the backyard. "Dude, we all know you and Jackie are fucking. You might as well call it what it is and stop this bullshit sneaking around."

"I've known her since I was five, we're just close."

"Don't do that, don't lie about it. Not to me. Seriously. You're just scared to admit it 'cause part of you still thinks it's wrong."

"I don't wanna talk about it, okay? You're right, but let it go. Leave it alone."

"Fine. But you're not being fair to Jackie."

He zippered into his tent, sprawled on the sleeping bag. I knew he was trying to find the balance between considering me a friend and a pursuit, wanting to find the space in which he could fit himself that would keep me close without interference. He knew me as part of a pair, found me that way in the middle of the desolate west, built his idea of me from stories pieced out from both my mouth and Jackie's. We shared our stories with him as we did each other - overlapping memories made full by each other's repeated details. Determining the start and end of the lines that sketched Jackie and me together couldn't be easy.

At the end of the summer, I loosened, acknowledged our partnership out into public, affectionate with Jackie at home in Bruce's backyard. Arcata opened and closed itself to me, enlarging as we explored but narrowing in scope. The city was stagnant, everything in existence for cash with no other way to spend. People talking about making enough then leaving, but no one ever moved. How do you leave a guaranteed six-figure income when you abandoned school and career to obtain it? You've been self-employed as a euphemism—*landscaper, gardener*—for too long now. And, where else will you find yourself with hours of free time and the money to finance it?

Jackie and I got breakfast out each Sunday morning to routine our lives, to keep a sense of the days that blended one to the next. With little responsibility but to show up with scissors, we barely observed weekends. For the first time, we weren't required to spend our morning off listening to a pastor admonish us to be wary. Every day was a weekend, so we replaced church with another form of socialization.

We benched ourselves at the long counter at Renata's Creperie, the tables almost always full by the time we arrived, Bloody Marys to kick off our week. The bartender trimmed weed with us and wasn't worried about our age. The others who surged through the restaurant were consistent, rarely a new voice behind us as I ate a savory crepe and Jackie sipped her drink and forked around the lettuce of her salad, rarely bringing bite to mouth. Sometimes I could convince her to eat a slice of dry toast or share a bowl of muesli from the café up the street. Mostly, she lived off of an occasional apple or Lara Bar. Still, we frequented restaurants, listening to the conversations surrounding us as much as talking.

"No, ketchup is a fact of life!" asserted an HSU student, indignant at his friend's claims against the value of high-fructose corn syrup condiments.

"But dude, Heinz makes it all natural now and it still tastes like shit."

We laughed, jotted down memories of the bizarre statements that seemed to define the city.

Our overheard conversations allowed me substitute interactions for the connections I was craving. Without classes or work to put me in touch with people outside of the growers' circle that adopted us, and too shy to initiate random interactions at the park or stores, I had no way to make new friends. My world consisted of Luke, Bruce and Dustin. And Jackie. But the inevitable complication of friend to lover between us left me without a close girlfriend or a confidante. My life was bordered in like the square Plaza in the city. The four blocks, Luke, Bruce, Dustin and Jackie. They were the buildings lining them to keep me centered to the small space.

Jackie pulled me to the redwood grove whenever we fought, banded me to the same tree. Breathed the dampness of the forest across my neck to calm me. She'd steal me there at dusk as people left the park and fumble our way home through the dark after we'd inhaled enough of age and each

other to satisfy our anger down to annoyed. Early morning
tented, we'd smell like earth in our sleeping bag.

T
HE EARTHQUAKE JARRED through early evening in
late summer. I was chopping cilantro and fresh tomatoes in the kitchen as Jackie knifed and scooped
avocados. Dustin and Bruce were rearranging the living
room, spacing out the floor to allow more people to stand.
Bruce had sent Luke off on a daylong errand list to get him
out of the house while we decorated for his surprise party. He
was turning twenty-four, older than I'd guessed when we first
met and discussed college. We rigged up speakers through the
house and into the backyard. There was carne asada mar-
inated in the refrigerator, ready for the grill. Bags of chips,
piles of fresh tortillas, and shredded red cabbage lined the
kitchen table, along with precooked rice in bowls ready to be
reheated. Jackie moved on from guacamole prep to make a
sauce. I set the chef's knife on the edge of the cutting board
and lightly whipped her backside with a rolled up towel. She
turned to kiss me.

The framed photograph of Barcelona hanging in the kitch-
en fell first. Crashed glass skittered beneath my feet as I tried
to balance against the uncertain counters. Jackie grabbed me,

clutching down my shoulder as I tried to react but froze. Bruce yelled in, something about doorways, windows. I saw Dustin lean against the frame that separated the rooms, slide down to sitting. The sill by the sink shifted and the window shattered into the basin as the refrigerator door uncorralled mustard, jars of pickles, and left over cranberry quinoa salad to run across the floor. Another picture fell, a side table with a loose leg lost balance. Hangers swung coats to the floor of the closet. The Tibetan prayer flags strung across the doorway fluttered. A wineglass crashed out of the cabinet. The radio silenced.

The shaking lasted twenty-five seconds. Bruce googled the quake on his phone, checking the official seismological society website. The quake registered a 6.2 on the Richter scale. Jackie ran to the bathroom and returned with a wet washcloth, Neosporin and a handful of band-aids. I noticed three drops of blood on my shirt and pulled a small piece of glass from where it stuck to my cheek. She washed my face and covered where the window had scattered across my nose and forehead. Dustin began sweeping up the glass.

"Somebody call Luke," I mumbled.

The power stayed out and we walked to Wildberries, the local grocery store, to buy candles with the rest of the town. Bruce fielded calls from the invited partygoers and assured everyone the grill still had gas, coolers still had ice, and he still had alcohol and weed. Why cancel? Luke wasn't answering his phone, but Bruce insisted he'd sent him all over and the reception was shitty in lots of areas. We listened to the radio in Bruce's truck, argued about how seriously to take the tidal wave warnings. The earthquake's epicenter was out in the ocean, just thirty miles off the coast of Eureka.

"We had a bigger earthquake a couple years ago and they ordered evacuation. My friends went out surfing, thinking they'd catch some massive waves. Dude, nothing."

"But what if it was farther out in the ocean that time? What if we ignore it and it ends up…" I'd never felt the earth beneath me shake. The uncertainty of the ground felt even more unnerving than the green of the sky before the midwest tornadoes I'd grown up witnessing.

"Jesus, do you ever stop worrying?"

We heard from Luke an hour later. He was driving when the quake started. His truck shook around the road, two cars in front of him collided and twisted across, blockading the street in both directions. No injuries. A bridge on a side road he tried to take had crumbled, the foundation dislodged from the cement that held it together. Downed trees scattered branches across the road, over a power line. But most houses and buildings appeared intact. Little structural damage apart from shattered glass that would soon be fixed. The shaking would be relegated to collective story for those present, and erased otherwise, sinking back into the earth that rose and fell.

Luke arrived home fifteen minutes after the power came back on to find the house full of friends and loose associations. We yelled *Surprise!* out of ritual obligation, passed him a beer and started grilling. He smiled and slapped Bruce on the back, joked around with Dustin. I slipped into the kitch-en, wanting to be occupied, busying myself with assembling tacos by the open space where the window had been. My hands shook and I couldn't hold a knife to chop more toma-toes. Luke propped himself against the counter after dodging the guests.

"I'm okay, you know. Go hang out with people," I said.

"Nah, I'd rather chill in here. Everyone's just swapping stories about where they were when the big one hit. Did you make the marinade?"

"Yeah, just a recipe from Epicurious."

"Thanks for the party. But, you better have gotten choco-late cake, or I'm leaving."

"Chocolate with chocolate mousse filling and chocolate ganache. I'm going to cure you of your addiction through over-saturation."

"Never." Luke leaned his forehead against the front of my shoulder, dangling a beer in his right hand, left hand palmed to counter. "I'm worried about you."

"I'm good, Jackie's good, work's good. What's to worry about?" I rinsed and toweled my hands, leaned into them on the edge of the sink.

"The food thing's her deal. You can't save her and it's not your fault."

"I know."

"You say that, but I don't think you do. I know whatever you two are figuring out about your relationship is none of my business. I can stand by and be supportive and keep my jealousy to myself. I can do that for you. But I don't want you to take on Jackie's problems." He kept his head down as he spoke, anchoring us both, non-threatening. "I hear you guys fight. Tents aren't exactly soundproof."

I stared out the window at the backyard, where our three-tent itinerant triangle usually stood, moving and expanding when new friends rolled through, shrinking back to base when they left. We'd worn brown spots of grass into the yard under the footprints that normally lay anchored by metal stakes. With the camp dismantled and stored for the party, the spots resembled crop circles and people unconsciously avoided the brown grass, never standing in the dead patches but arranging bodies around them.

"I'd better go play nice with the party guests." Luke grabbed a fresh beer and left me hunched and staring.

Earth shaking, while trying to stand, still feels like night-time after a day in a wave pool or on an active ocean. Even as you lie still in bed, you feel the movements around you, feel yourself pulled and pulsed around by a force you can't stop. For weeks after the earthquake, I felt the ground moving beneath me. I couldn't tell if I was imagining another event or if I'd somehow become more attuned to the slight shifts below my feet. Every time a picture fell or a can dropped off a shelf in the grocery store, I braced myself against a wall or ran to a doorway. I was always aware of windows.

I began recurring dreaming every night. The earth begins to quiver, slow-motion shaking to the rhythm of an old Rolling Stones record my mother used to play, a remnant of her secular life with my father. I run to the edge of the cornfields by Jackie's house and see the rows folding out, parting to the beat of *Satisfaction*. Jackie is on the other side, carrying Danny in her arms and yelling soundlessly for me to follow. As I reach the first stalks, Jackie appears behind me, skin falling off her slowly as the old Jackie runs ahead with Danny. I chase into the rows, the skeleton stepping out of her skin and reaching toward me. Danny climbs down ahead, sprints farther and farther in front of me as the stalks swish shut, closing me in a shifting folded bubble. I lose my way in the corn, rows curving and rearranging in circles. The ground jolts, opens. Swigs me down into its gaping, trembling mouth. I woke sweating and smelling parsley.

After Luke's party, I stopped trying to convince Jackie to eat. Worry shook through me, but I contained it, tried to show Luke I listened and knew the validity of what he said. But I couldn't extract myself from Jackie. We'd spent too many years together breathing the same stories, knowing the same families, friends, adventuring the same new spaces. Now, loving her was a conflict in itself but also a promise, and allowing her to devour herself pained my stomach as much as her hunger ached hers.

Out to dinner, we celebrated Jackie's nineteenth birthday, ignoring the silence of Danny, avoiding acknowledging the passing of a year since his suicide. Virgin cocktails, Jackie taking small sips, trying to pass off as drinking much more than she was. When I offered the basket of small rolls, she pulled one into tiny bites, spread the pieces over her plate and moved them around like a magician shuffling peas under cups for a trick. She caught my eye and pushed a piece into her mouth, chewing in equal progressions like a metronome, bite, up, bite, up. When she thought I looked away, she slipped her napkin up and spit the roll into it.

We played our eyes around the restaurant, making inane comments about the decorations and other patrons, the menu. After years of chattering through our lives together, we'd reached an odd space of silence. Whether we'd exhausted our connection or complicated it to the point of closing off, I wasn't sure. Jackie's mind seemed to dwell exclusively in reference to food—whether a leaf of lettuce should count for 100 or 200 calories, if Pepsi was actually adding sugar to its diet pop—and mine circled around guessing and interpreting her thoughts, wanting to reteach her, save her. Feed her.

Our food arrived and she sent the plate back, saying the still steaming fish wasn't hot enough. The waiter puzzled his brow at me, as if asking a parent if he needed to indulge the child. I shrugged. When he returned with the food, the fish visibly rubbery and slightly shrunken, Jackie demanded a bottle of mustard. I watched as she doused the entire plate—fish, asparagus, potatoes—in yellow and shook pepper until no more would come out. When she stood to grab a pepper grinder from another table, I grasped her wrist.

"Seriously, Jackie!" She turned toward my hiss and glared.

"It's not my fault they don't know how to keep pepper shakers full," she said, intending for the server to hear.

"You've used so much already you can't even see the food. Sit down."

I pulled at her arm, afraid of how weak she'd become, embarrassed by my desire to force her to eat. She wrenched out of my grip, grabbed her plate and sat at an empty table across the room. I apologized to the waiter, paid our bill and shrank past other diners.

"You don't get to tell me how to eat!" she screamed after me.

Outside, I glanced back through the large picture window and saw Jackie tapping the table with one hand as she stared at the food she cut into smaller and smaller pieces with her fork. The mustard and fish, asparagus and red potatoes, speckled over with pepper reminded me of a Pollack painting, Jackie's stare comparable to any artist lost in his work.

She crawled into our tent around midnight. I'd fallen asleep moments before, after spending several hours curled up against Luke, loosing my tears on his white t-shirt, letting him tell me, over and over, that I wasn't responsible for Jackie. Trying to believe him. We shared half a bottle of tequila left over from the party and he carried me to my sleeping bag. As he tucked me in, unzippering the two bags Jackie and I hooked together and re-designating a separate space for me, I was overwhelmed with memories of Danny. Black hair falling in eyes as he leaned over me, folded blankets around us. Hands that held my head to the earth as we camped in fields for hours we tried to stretch to days. Luke kissed my forehead goodnight and I couldn't distinguish him from the memories. When Jackie inchwormed her way to me, I woke in half-drunk groggy daze and thought Danny had reappeared.

Jackie tried to whisper sorry but I rolled away from her, flopped myself as far to the nylon edge of our home as I could, stomached to the ground. She unzipped my bag and I thrashed. But she unpackaged me and I wondered how her hands could grip so tightly as she yanked me from the tent. I followed her, wondering why I always tagged after, silently cursing myself for not yelling or running to Luke's tent. She would kiss me, run her hands around me, a trigger for forgiveness she flicked again and again.

As she pulled me toward the redwoods, I replayed our previous pattern. Slivers of bark inching around my toes, my sandals thinning where my feet imprint steps each day, small rocks pressing up against my heels. She escaped me here to reroot in me, grow herself through me so I wouldn't let go. The sensation of bark to back and needles soft-pricking thighs, moss velveting up arms and under feet. Words seem too loud there, even when whispered, and she said nothing as her shadow slipped us up to the clearing.

We stumbled with no flashlight, the waxing moon not enough, wondering if we'd lost our way. Jackie knew the path in ways I never did, an internal sense of direction combined with walks I suspected she took daily as exercise and avoidance. The old stump and tree cluster should have been to our left. But we found a mass of tumbled trees jungle-gymming over the spot instead. Half-unearthed roots where trees leaned across. We could crawl into the cove's base, military-slither ourselves under the crisscross of trunks above. But there was no room to contort ourselves back together, patterned in the brief shards of light that made their way through the covering overhead. When I reached out my fingers to slide up the skin of the tree where we first kissed, I scraped knuckles against the rough hide of a new, younger tree.

I weaseled my body out of the freshly caved ground and began walking toward home. Jackie called after me but I refused to answer, refused to turn around. She begged, talked of clearing the newly fallen trunks, recreating our retreat. I left her standing there, crying, and yelling about climbing higher over the branches like a ladder, reaching us out of the city.

Jackie spent a week away from Bruce's and our little camp. None of us saw her, no one knew where she went. One evening I came home to find her sleeping bag missing. She skipped a trimming job. Luke was less concerned for her than for me, asking around town if people had seen her, in order to comfort me rather than to find Jackie. Someone mentioned a young girl living in the redwood park, bumming joints and wandering around off trail. I left a small cooler of food at the base of the tree cove, taped a note telling her we were worried to the sleeping bag poking out from below the fallen trunks. I tried not to think about how easily the trees could dislodge and crumble into the crawlspace below.

She came back to grab her bag of clothes and the cash she kept in Bruce's safe, to tell us she'd found an apartment and roommate and would be moving immediately. I figured she'd found the place from one of the index cards handwritten with a number and brief description—*cozy, clean, 420-friendly*—tacked to the bulletin board in Wildberries' entryway. Maybe she met someone in the park, made conversation as she listened to him playing an acoustic guitar, mentioned her homeless shelter in the grove. I clenched teeth down on my tongue until I tasted blood, switched to my lip as I watched her move through the house, the tent, packing herself out of our make-shift home. When she walked away and I moved to chase, Luke cuffed my waist and held me back. My elbow to his ribs and still he held, pinning my sides with his arm.

Luke slept in my tent that night, weighted me to the ground as I dreamt again of earthquakes, Jackie multiplied and dying as she chased me. The dream shifted and her skeleton reached me before the earth devoured me, yanked me further into the field, tried to kiss me as I stared at the hollows where her eyes had been. I pulled down dried stalks of corn, covered her, reinvented her skin with crumbling husks.

JACKIE NO LONGER ANSWERED HER PHONE. I didn't know if she screened against me or if her mind had trailed so far away from itself that ringing no longer registered as a cue. Within a month of leaving, she was working at a local café, drawn to the food she denied herself. I imagined the people buying pastries from her, women walking in for a piece of cake or a chocolate croissant, feeling guilty and jealous at the sight of Jackie, thoughts jumping to their thighs, the calories in the food they crave. Their orders coming out involuntarily as a single macaron instead of turtle cheesecake or the raspberry mousse. I considered walking down from our camp, pretending an errand for Luke's lunch or mid-afternoon coffee, but I was afraid of cornering her, forcing a meeting. Had I known her roommate, I would have called, asked her to yell Jackie over to the phone, known for sure if she were home.

Instead, I went to a stationary store downtown, a tiny shop lined with boxes of pages, potential reunions or elegies. Plastic shelves on plywood frames held a library of cards with few repeats. Old postcards were shuffled in with the rest, boxed

sets of reprint watercolors, local artists' work cardstocked
along with classics. The shop owner was overly helpful, cus-
tomer-starved and eager to help me discover just the right
image expression.

"What can I help you find? We have some lovely birthday
cards and stationary. Oh! Let me show you our new collection of invitations!"

I apologized him away, telling him I'd come to him with
any questions. He resigned to his swivel chair behind the
counter with the *Cash Only* sign and watched my oversized
shoulder bag as I weaved around the shelves. Choosing the
perfect card seemed a grail search, as though finding the right
visual and preprinted word combination would unlock Jackie
to me. My fingers shifted through column and row, scanning
each card that passed my first glances. When I exhausted the
collection, I shuffled back through, hoping to catch one that
I missed, one that had fallen between the shelves. But no card
could encompass all I wanted, so I settled on an off-white
textured card with a photograph of the ocean hitting the cliffs
in Trinidad. The inside was blank.

On impulse, I purchased a box of white stationary with a thin
blue border that was propped up near the register. The owner
raised his eyebrows and examined the box like a fine wine, de-
claring my choice solid, "Crane makes fine stationary." When
he asked me with whom I'd be corresponding, I grabbed the
card and box, threw my cash on the counter and walked out.

I folded myself onto a bench in the Plaza, watched a group
of students from Dell'Arte contorting themselves over the

concrete bricks, clowning for the crowd of smokers spread out on blankets. My compulsion to write Jackie seemed increasingly foolish as I flipped words around my mind, never lingering on any long enough to find what I was trying to say. I could pen down sentences to jar her, try to wake her from the hunger-induced daze I'd seen her shifting in around town. But when I imagined her reading a letter wishing her to eat, I remembered months before when even trail mix was enough to start silent wars, and I didn't want to drive her further from sight.

My mind kept jumping back to Danny, wondering what he would say to a sister that wouldn't eat. He would coax food into her, convince her a turkey sandwich was the thing he most wanted her to have and she'd devour it like manna. But if he were here, she wouldn't fight food anyway. We'd be running across the plains or the campus of a local college, the three of us schooled into the four-year plan our parents created for us. Unaware that the plains ended and life began in different elevations.

So I wrote her an update, as if she'd gone away on vacation for a month and I was catching her up on what she'd missed. I synopsized the movies I'd rented recently and the preseason football games I'd watched at the Arcata Theater Lounge with the guys. How Bruce said at least 70 percent of the theater crowd was comprised of growers. Wrote of the extra large crop Bruce had produced and how it took us more than a week to get through it. Of the strange sensation of waking alone and thinking she would be there.

*We shuffled the camp around. Our old tent started leak-
ing, so I bought a new one and set it up closer to the door. I
still eat two eggs, toast and orange juice for breakfast. I don't
know how to keep pretending I'm okay without you around,
Jackie. We've shared too many years for this silence. I'll apologize a thousand times over if you will just call me.*

I realized the letter was more for me than for Jackie, a way
to process through the situation, arrive myself at a half-com-
fort. If I heard from her I would be thrilled, but I didn't expect
a response.

JACKIE CALLED ME WHILE I WAS TRIMMING, my phone buzz-
ing in my purse and I couldn't reach for it with the resin
sticking up my fingers. When I called her back, Jackie's déjà
vu voice, unburdened with anger or annoyance, returned me
to summer. She spoke as though we'd never stopped talking,
she back from her trip, ready to hang out again.

"Sorry it took me so long to get back to you, love. Thanks
for the letter, it was so sweet. Let's get coffee soon, yeah?"

Slipping back into communication with Jackie, I wanted
to guard myself against her, but couldn't. When we met for
coffee and she told me her roommate would be moving out
at the end of the month, my first impulse was to ask if I could
take her place. She suggested it before I could mention the
idea and I paused, committed to a maybe, let-me-check-my-
finances, half-yes. Part of me felt certain that a more stable
living situation – bed and kitchen and bathroom of our own,

no more sleeping on the ground covered only by thin nylon when the rains came – would ease the problems between us, allow us the space and comfort we lacked before. But even a month and Jackie had thinned, her fingers narrow as pipe cleaners, soft white hair growing up her neck and around her face, her body angled into the chair and shifting every few seconds. She could barely keep eye contact. I wrapped myself around her frame, her shoulders digging into my arms, promised her a definite answer within a week.

EOPLE FLOCKED TO HUMBOLDT. A natural growth
gold rush. Luke told me even the cigarette companies
had begun buying up tracts of land in Northern California. Anticipation. Young adults, students, middle-agers
looking for a fresh start. A few bucks for start-up costs. A
connection helped. Entire towns on a cash-only basis. Everyone owned a *landscape* business or worked a service job in a
store that only existed because of an overabundance of people
with expendable income and too much free time. Schools sent
home notes with students asking parents to brush the trim off
of their children's backpacks and shoes. The locals laughed
at the films made about the county. The documentaries and
exposés—called one or the other depending on the network
owner funding the show—that all tried to portray a rebel-
lious or semi-legal or fuck-you attitude of growers, failed to
understand the communities. Failed to recognize the attitude
existed only in the pride of being forerunners, of cultivating a
substance less damaging than legal drugs that remained polit-
ically vilified. A medicine and recreation that threatened the
pulp and paper and alcohol industries. People sat and smoked

in public and the cops only bothered the too-aggressive pan-handlers. Employees talked about strains at work, people carried papers and jars with them, growers discussed business in public. Not to flaunt or rebel. Just because it was natural. Part of things. Not everyone burned, but nobody cared.

After five months in the area, I no longer considered smoking in public bizarre, never gave the obvious odor of herb on clothes a second thought. The presence of marijuana was no more out of the ordinary than a Bible on a coffee table back in Iowa. At the end of each day we barbecued, built a fire and camped out in Bruce's backyard. Luke started sharing my tent after Jackie moved to town.

"We should get an apartment before the winter," Luke said. "It doesn't get super cold, but the rains start and a tent won't be so great."

I flopped onto my back and half-smiled at him. The idea of moving in together excited me, but I couldn't tell if it stemmed from living with Luke, or simply the idea of sending my mother a letter describing the apartment I shared with a boyfriend. I imagined her bursting into tears, calling her pastor's wife, praying every night that I would come home.

"Yeah? How long do you want to stay out here? I mean, what'll we do once the season's over?"

"There's always work. I'll get a job in town or something, we'll figure it out." He bent over and kissed my neck. "Stick with me, Baby, and you'll never have to worry," he teased. I laughed and pulled him down.

"Yeah, yeah. I kinda told Jackie I'd move in with her when

her roommate moves out of their place next month. But I'll think about it, okay?"

"What's to think about? You and Jackie barely talk anymore. Babe, she's losing it, getting too caught up with her damn weight. Bruce pulled strings for her on that job and she never even showed. Didn't even call Tim to let him know."

Luke was right. I wanted to hold onto Jackie as I knew her before, clutching at her through shared coffees, a shared apartment. But when I imagined living with her I didn't see a small apartment in Arcata. Instead, the plains opened in front of me, a yellow farmhouse with a porch that wrapped around in white paint, old wide wooden planks across the kitchen floor. Jackie standing in a bedroom, switching dresses on and off of her full frame, soft belly, thighs and arms with weight she held onto rather than sloughed off as quickly as starving would allow.

"Let's look for a place this weekend," I said, knowing Luke would wake me the next morning, untent me and take me to breakfast. We'd grab a copy of the local paper and browse the ads for apartments, circle possibilities in black pen, make calls as we sipped our coffee. He was as impulsive as I'd felt when leaving Iowa, but all the time. Never thinking long-term, never considering if he'd want the same things a month later. Every time I hesitated, he had a reason why I shouldn't, usually boiling it down to me needing to stop worrying or just go with it. In agreeing to bunk with him, I was trying both to let go of Jackie and to reinvent myself. Around Luke I needed to be someone different, break myself into another person, or at least shut off parts of me. I'd saturate myself with his philosophy, his overly relaxed approach. We'd build our own religion out of not investing faith in anything, worship ourselves daily in each other and discover how far we could push our bodies to intensity.

I INTENDED TO TELL JACKIE ABOUT LUKE. But when we met for coffee, I explained financial struggles, wanting to save more, not being ready to commit to another year leased into Arcata. My words staccatoed out of my mouth and I figured she knew I was excusing my way around the real reason. Her face never registered betrayal or wounded, and I realized she barely remembered offering me the place.

"Oh, well that works out great, then. Anna found someone else to take her spot anyway. She's moving in tomorrow."

"Sounds like you've got it figured out, I guess." I tried to hide the choked tears in my voice, feeling replaced. I didn't want Jackie, not exactly. I knew I couldn't live with her, that every pound she lost would destroy me, that we'd fight and bicker as I tried to resurrect us as before, but I didn't want to share her with a stranger. I wanted her to pine for me, to crave me as she had even when Danny and I shared each other to her exclusion.

"How are you and Luke doing?" When I stared at her she whispered, "Dustin told me. Thought I should know."

"He's not you, Jackie. He's..." My tongue clicked at the roof of my mouth, trying to force out appropriate words. But

I hadn't defined Luke to myself or myself to him and couldn't explain to Jackie that his hands felt different, less exciting but safe, uncontroversial.

She stood, kissed my cheek, walked out the door and across the Plaza. Her legs seemed to pop, joint themselves around her hips as she walked, and I tried to imagine the ache of underfed bone. She'd lost all fluidity, lurching around as she shivered herself through the town.

THE ONLY BAR IN BLUE LAKE is small-time famous. Logging equipment serves as wallpaper, ceiling tiles. Axes, hand saws, two-people tooth-bladed six foot strips of handled metal. I sat at the bar always manned by the same gruff bartender and wondered what she would do if a fight broke out. To my side, a few guys I knew peripherally from town played pool. Three growers I'd worked for and their girlfriends covered a table with beer bottles. About ten feet from the neon jukebox a woman swayed her hips, not rhythmically dancing or trying to catch the drummer's thump. Hair swinging, hands shaking, elbows twitching. I waited for her to lift her face, wanted her eyes on mine. I'd never seen her before.

She drank scotch straight-up, swallowed without gagging or face-reflecting the burn. Ordered a second glass as she countered the empty, regulars along the bar impressed. She stood near me as she leaned on the counter and I wanted to stare, but ran my eyes to dust-dim lights and webbed rafters, the first dollar earned tacked to the wall behind the register, old tapped beer handles with taped-on pieces of notebook paper sharpied with the new name.

The music stopped and she kept swaying. A man stumbled over and grabbed her waist, tried to keep to her motion but couldn't catch her rhythm. She didn't flinch when he touched her, or when he let go. I imagined mumbling in her ear, a flirtatious concentration-break, but I slid onto a tattered stool closer by, instead. Her earthy perfume reminded me of camp and I wanted to bury my nose in her neck and breathe until I felt home. When the gap in the music reached her ears she looked at me, startled to the jukebox then the bar, fished her hands in her pockets.

She nodded to the bartender and left without paying. I wanted to chase her through the parking lot and ask her to follow me somewhere we didn't know. Some town where I was no strict mother's daughter, no fear-product of upbringing. Some place where I could allow myself to love a woman.

Hours later, cabbed home with one of the pool players, I was tongued over and squirmed against, legs flipped, synapsed to bed nerves firing to the rhythm of alcohol coursing. He clenched his fist around my wrist as he snored and dizzying into sleep I saw the woman. I caught her outside the bar, pressed a quarter to her palm and told her to go back in, to pick a song that wouldn't end. A song long enough to propel us from the dive. She pressed 11-07 and we danced our hip arm bone rhythms and collapsed into an empty field, woke drenched like grass with dew and started our tapping across the plain.

I NEVER APOLOGIZED TO LUKE after nights when I didn't come home and never worried about creating an excuse. He never asked. He just pulled me into the bedroom when I arrived, undressed me, watched me lie still as he reclaimed me. Sometimes he'd stay in bed while I made dinner or left for a job. Other times he'd lock himself in his studio, music blaring from his stereo as he painted.

We pooled our money, bought our groceries together, shared a car. I washed dishes and he took our clothes to the laundromat up the street. We designated dates each week—wine bar, movie, camping up north, trips to Seattle, Portland, Napa. When the sex dulled, we watched porn, bought toys, invented games. We tried.

At night I watched Luke sleep, toss from facing me to back turned, bare ribs expanding as he sighed out snores. When I curled next to him I felt further away, as though the closer our bodies got to touching the more the distance between us was exaggerated. When I left for work or coffee in the morning, I left him still sleeping next to the indented shape of me that had settled into semi-permanent. I imagined him caressing its outline on the nights when I stayed away, tracing my absence over the sheets with two fingers as if wondering whether I were real or a made up memory of a warm body pulsing beside him. He noses my pillowcase, trying to trigger the rush of recognition fastened to a person's scent, rubs his cheek against the sheets, flips a leg over the spot where my hips should be.

Each morning he told me he loved me, every day he repeated it through voicemails and notes left around the apartment. But he continued to withdraw and I kept seeking myself in other men, searching for a satisfaction I associated with new sheets. The thrill of fitting into a new person overshadowed the comfort of Luke and home. Despite his spontaneity, his whims that switched the course of his future plans daily but he would never implement, he reminded me of boredom, of the unsettling feeling of being trapped in someone else's plan.

I wanted to call Jackie, wanted to grab her and run up the coast, reinvent ourselves together again. Buy a car older than ourselves, rusting welded seams barely containing the seats inside. Click and clunk our way up the winding roads. Jackie would love Portland and we could settle into a small loft downtown, cheap-print art the walls and soundtrack our lives with acoustic and indie. She'd work in a coffee shop and I'd waitress or sit at a front desk greeting people, we'd sell the car for scrap and bicycle everywhere. Enroll in some classes, group ourselves with an itinerant young crowd, move across the city en masse to discover new cafés. We'd rename ourselves and map a new day-to-day in the overcast streets.

Sometimes I'd catch glimpses of her in town, spectral wisps darting around a corner. She continued to lose weight, her face gaunt, aged to seventies at only nineteen. When I saw her up close she flickered recognition behind papery skin that clutched across the hollow between cheekbone and chin, but she seemed clouded, unable to hold onto my image, and never said hello. In high school I'd been fascinated by how we move, the earth propelling us forward in reaction to our pressure against it. As Jackie shifted herself across the street I wondered how she created enough force with her weight to beckon the ground to push one step to the next.

I MONOLOGUED WITH MY MOTHER through ambivalent letters written on the Crane stationary. Never started with *Dear*, but jumped right into a rant or summary of the week, folded and cross-countried the stories with a friend going east or south so the postmark changed every time. Envelopes sent with no return address. In one note I named the creperie and soon a pile of letters my mother had written but not known where to send arrived at the restaurant. I read her letters in batches, saving four or five for a winter afternoon when the rain creeped through the windowsills.

She still lived in the farmhouse with images of her ex-husband and daughter framed and scattered on mantles, tables, bookcase shelves. A man from church took her out to dinner a few times a month, drove her to Chicago for the weekend to see an opera or browse the museums, played weekly games of bridge as her partner. He asked her to think about marriage but she refused, unresolved loyalty clasping her to a family that she increasingly realized wouldn't return. *I don't know how to let go*, she wrote, and for the first time I could relate to my mother. She processed through my absence in her writing, moving through denial and anger and grief in the way we forgot to do with Danny. The earlier letters threatened, manipulated me home, then moved to asking for a visit, and, finally, to wishing me well. She included a photocopied Bible page with each letter, with a verse highlighted or underlined, scrawled side-lined notes from years of rereading the book showing up faded in the reprint.

Every time I read a letter, her image floated before me; hunched back, desked at her side table, old oversized scarf draped around her shoulders with the folds so carelessly perfect I could never imitate the style. Three pens paralleled as backups, the fourth scratching across the page in level arcs. Her handwriting artistic enough that it justified particular pens, scratchy thin-inked implements that rendered her words extra delicate. Growing up, I'd spent hours trying to mimic her writing, but my words lurched onto pages in clumpy, almost illegible print. Cursive was beyond my motor control. She alone could resurrect the dying letter, refusing to make much use of her e-mail account even as her friends from high school stopped writing, insisting they didn't have time to sit down to anything but a computer. She kept an old oil lantern next to the bed, in case of a power outage. I imagined she lit it whenever she wrote, the light flickering words to her, transmitting a timelessness to the pages.

I relegated the photographs she sent to the small fireproof, waterproof safe I kept tucked in the closet. New pictures of Iowa–a redecorated bathroom, the especially large zucchini from the garden, a hummingbird that visited the feeder each day–and old family photos lay on top of my passport and medical marijuana certificate. Sometimes I thought of sending her a box of cookies made with weed butter just to see what type of letters she'd write when her mind released itself from the controlled edges into which she fenced it. But as much as I loathed her dogma, I needed her to represent strict consistency. Even as I practiced saying *Jesus Christ!* in annoyance, *fuck* as a barely-swear, I needed to imagine her indignant, ready to spank the daughter—who now rose taller than she did—to remind her of the consequence of words. She was a bearing to the life I'd given up, a reminder of why I wanted out. If she ate a weed cookie and called to say, *goddamn this unbearable heat!*, my world would unhinge and I would convince myself I was stuck in a bad trip. A childhood melting in front of me from a compound word I hardly noticed until it fell out of her mouth.

I wanted to edit her letters to include the parts she left out. When she weekended in Chicago with Mark, did they book separate hotel rooms, sleep on twin beds separated by an aisle wide enough to keep things to her doctrine? Did she still follow the rules she set for me? I grabbed a red pen and marked the margins to ask what I wanted noted on the day they arrived, what I craved hearing or built as mother from a distance. But a rewritten, relaxed parent would be no better than the parables I grew up with, stories to feed a need for comfort, an easy-listening station of morality. She remained forever the person I wanted to convert away and needed to keep indoctrinated.

WHEN I WALKED THROUGH THE DOOR, still high-heeled and in full mascara, eye shadow smudged to lids, Luke stayed sitting on the couch, beer in hand even at eleven. Smashed bits of the glass tabletop mosaicked on the floor. I dropped my purse on the kitchen counter and eased around the shards to stand facing him. Luke kept his eyes focused down on the edge of the fake Oriental rug peeking out from below the table.

"What's his name this time, or do you even remember?"

"It doesn't matter."

"Tell me his goddamn name."

"Alex." I lied. His real name was fuzzed somewhere to the back spaces of my brain and I didn't want to spend the time trying to summon it. We hadn't exchanged numbers when I left. He was a placeholder.

"Was he good?"

"Why does it matter to you?"

"Answer the fucking question. Did he make you come?"

"Yes."

"More than once?"

"Stop this."

"Did he make you orgasm more than once?"

"Seriously, stop."

"Did he go down on you?"

"Luke, stop it."

"Did you like how he fucked you? Was he better than me?"

When I refused to answer, he threw his beer bottle across the room. The glass bounced into pieces, beer sudsing in a drip trio down the wall. I moved for paper towels but paused at his low grumble. He stood, taller by only a couple inches but rising higher now than I'd known he could. Stepped toward me, I backed to wall. In soccer practice, my coach taught me to watch the hips for indicative movements, that arms and legs deceive but pelvis shows you the path of the motioned body. I stared at his belt as he crunched over the glass on the floor.

"Why are you cowering in the corner? Do you really think I'd hit you?" he whispered at me. "After all these men, I'm still here, and you think now I'd decide to throw a punch?"

"I don't know why, Luke, I don't know why I can't be satisfied..."

He dropped to the floor in front of me, wrapped an arm up my thigh and one around my ankles, leaned his head to my knees. Gentle seemed an odd word for drunk-slammed bottles and a cuckolded man, but when I looked at Luke that was all I saw. I needed him to get angry with me, fury spilling out the way it would from my lips and fists if I'd been cheated on and neglected. But he whispered when he should scream and I had no defense for it.

"I'm sorry, Baby," I fingered through his hair. "Please, give me another shot. I'll try. This time, I'll really try."

"You're breaking me."

"I know. I'm so, so sorry. Please…" I didn't know what to plead for, didn't know whether I wanted him to stay or walk out. "Please, just don't…"

He slid his chin above my kneecap, bloodshot face searching me, waiting for sincerity to twitch across my eyes. I shut my lids and tilted head to ceiling, dripped a tear out of my left eye to my cheek, hoped my confusion and uncertainty would pass for remorse.

"If it happens again…" he trailed his gaze to the floor. "Just don't. Don't give me another reason to think it. If you're not happy, I'll let you go and we'll call it a good try and move on. Just have the decency to tell me before you run off."

I promised him into the shower because I knew no other way to relate to him. I washed away the night before, sprinkled water across both our foreheads and confessed to loving him. He soaped his hands around my skin, ran the water scalding over his face to hide his tears, pushed me against tile. As he moved in me I pressed my face against the grouted squares and considered the moldy scum penance for the night before, cheeked against the grime in repentance. He pulled my hair and I thought of Jackie by a lake, summer camp tanned and lean, ignoring the other girls as she pulled me deeper into the water. We gulped air and disappeared to touch the bottom of the lake as my body barely registered Luke groping me into the bedroom.

DANNY SOFTSPOKE HIS WAY through me while we dated, disarmed me in every argument with his failure to anger. Even after the forced miscarriage, while I baited him and begged him to end us, he calmed his way through every incitement. I wanted him to break up with me, felt he was justified to end our high school sweetheart status and I wasn't, believed if I provoked him enough, he would see I wasn't right for him. But he either convinced himself I was lifelong material or he obligated himself into staying together. Even when we drifted apart, when I held other hands and Jackie asked me, in front of him, how good a classmate was at kissing, he called me every night and still whispered *I love you* into my ear. When I finally couraged my way into the cornfields with him to make the end official, he nodded, knowing for months but waiting for a last goodbye. He hardly teared up, even as I sobbed.

As I lay in bed next to Luke, I ran my eyes down his silhouette, scared by the feeling that I couldn't distinguish him from Danny in the fogged moonlight that filtered over his right shoulder. They looked nothing alike, their voices were half-octaves different. Not knowing one from the other unnerved me, and I ceiling-stared through the nights trying to figure out why I couldn't tell them apart.

March 14

Dearest,

You know I would never do anything to upset you, as tentative as we are, eggshell walking and all. But I may have let your location slip to Jackie's father. He was drunk, I wasn't thinking. Sorry. Please don't be angry. He's been a wreck for months now. I don't think he has a job anymore. Jackie's mother stormed through here a few weeks ago to force him to sign divorce papers. She didn't even stop to say hello, can you believe that? After all those years.

Mark took me to Chicago again this weekend, made a whole show of fancy restaurants – can you believe some places charge over $25 just for a steak? – and buying me dresses and shoes. While we were sitting at the bar at the top of the Drake Hotel, overlooking the city and sipping cocktails (yes! your mother now has a cosmopolitan on special occasions), Mark pulled out a small blue box and knelt down on one knee to propose. It was all very romantic, and though I'd said no many times before when he'd approached the subject in casual conversation, I decided he is such a lovely part of my life already, and clearly cares about me, so I said yes.

I know we've never really discussed my life after your father, so I am not sure how this news will affect you. Please don't be angry with me. I am lonely and Mark treats me well. I feel like I deserve a little happiness, too. We plan to have a small wedding here in May. Please consider coming, it would mean a lot to me. You wouldn't have to stay long, only a day or two if you wanted. I wouldn't ask you anything you didn't want to answer. You could stand next to me as I got married, wouldn't that be a bit amusing? Not quite what God intended, I suppose, but He is gracious and merciful. You don't have to decide right away. Just promise to think about it.

On a side note, I am working on a new recipe for an apple pie to enter into the fair this fall. I even subscribed to some food magazines, to research some of the new trends in pies. Mostly, I've ended up clipping new recipes for chicken and beef, as I am always running out of new ways to prepare them. Sometimes I wish they'd invent another meat, or a new vegetable. Something to make dinner exciting again. Mark seems to like it when I try out some of the more exotic and gourmet dishes, and since he pays for the groceries anyway when I make dinner and doesn't seem to mind paying for things like truffle oil (can you believe people can get away with charging more than $70 dollars for a tiny bottle of oil?!) and ramps, I can experiment without guilt and I've become quite the self-taught chef. When you come for a visit sometime, we'll have to cook together. I bet living on the west coast has exposed you to all sorts of new and ethnic foods. How exciting!

I miss you. Come home soon. I promise not to try to convince you to stay. I just want to hug you again to make sure you're still real. You could meet Mark, we could go to dinner somewhere in town. I wouldn't even pry or ask about your love life. (But there must be someone, right?) Call me some-time soon if you feel up to it. You're in my prayers, always.

Love,
Mom

I REMEMBER MY MUSINGS. The way my mind dealt with the news of my mother's impending nuptials. The intermittent letters, her begging my presence, the feeling of dreading the mail arriving. I relive it, again and again, in my imagination of her:

My mother sends me clippings from the newspaper back home, sometimes whole sections black-smudged where thin creased paper rubbed against envelope over miles. I open an envelope to find the Midwest version of a society page: a black and white studio portrait, lit from both spotlight and fluorescent glow of mega-store warehouse lights, of my mother and plushy-faced Mark, arms all stiff-tangled around her shoulders. A blurb about ages and families, planned wedding month, location. His outline a grayscale sketch of monotony next to a spark even cheap photo sessions can't mute out of my mother's eyes.

I dart around the rest of the page, quick scan the obituaries, the myriad of young men and women in photographs. Everyone wants to be remembered as twenty-something and you have to read the write-ups to know if the photo indicates that they died tragically young or ripened to a sufficient age to feel a lesser grief. Mixed in with the obits and engagements I find clippings of weddings, announcements blurbed out for those refused an invitation.

"The bride wore fleece," and I imagine a hunter-orange vest over a crisp-ironed denim shirt, perhaps sunglasses pushed up the forehead to hold back her wavy brown hair, the groom in his Sunday-best Carhartt overalls bibbing-in a forest green and black plaid flannel shirt, both man and wife in tan boots with mud-darkened rubber feet. There's probably a gun in there somewhere, maybe a fired-off salute to the sky as the groom lips his neon-fleeced new wife. A potluck laid out by church wives—previous mentors with whom the woman rings and kisses her way into peerhood—tables across the church lawn all shepherd's pie and zucchini muffins and non-alcoholic punch floated with sherbet. Dogs run with children, nose food from their plates. Someone starts a bonfire as dusk hovers into the celebration and people sing a hymn after a group prayer over the couple. Smashed cake into faces tumbles onto clothes, the fleece dotted with crumbs of Duncan Hines vanilla-chocolate marble. Blue-ribbon pies spill from the church kitchen, apple and pumpkin and banana cream replacing the empty crockpots and roll baskets. Blankets from cars and metal chairs from the basement circle around the fire. The group hoots away the couple on a hay-covered wagon bed but the party continues into the warm summer night.

I place my mother in the image and laugh loud enough for Luke to cock his head from the Sunday crossword and wonder at me across the room. She eye-snickers at the scene, clutches my arm with slender proud fingers. I imagine her snide whispers, comments positioning herself in societal category of *higher*. She uses words like *slavering* to describe the children because she's read several recent books that include the phrase, even though she doesn't quite understand its meaning. The ladies from the church greet her distantly and she makes no effort to contribute. Her wedding will be so much more sophisticated. Did I know Mark had taken her to the opera and to a restaurant where they set each place with two forks and multiple wine glasses? Yes? Well of course she wrote to me about it. She would be wearing lace at her wedding, thank you.

My mother remains untouchable in her sense of pride, even in my daydreams. I memory-doll her into new scenes and bend her arms around different men, shear off her long hair and contact her eyes with blue lenses, clothe her in haute couture or reduce her to thrift-store eighties leftovers, but her mannerisms don't change. She stays solid in my mind, rigid backed to an upright Christian condescension. Loves her neighbors because she has to, does deeds that increase her credit with fellow churchgoers, and, oh yeah, that guy she worships, too. When she Bibles me with commandments, I disconnect the words from actions and mind-argue back that I really appreciated the kind thoughts, but I'm working on being happy with myself right now. If God could feel a little bit happier about my life, maybe I'd listen. In the meantime, I learned to play a few chords on an acoustic guitar and stopped sleeping around. I pretend she'd be proud if I told her this and cross *write Mom* off my to-do list for the day. Perhaps tomorrow will be better for placating. Or, I'll wake up, finally not giving a shit about offending my mother.

II

Jackie's father reached Arcata at dusk and sidewalked the nose of his car diagonally in the Plaza. He sloshed his way over the lawn, spinning in random ellipses as he tried to orient his way to his daughter. My mother, slowly building a location for the lost daughters from my letters, mentioned Arcata and a café to him one day when he rampaged across the lawn, a fifth of whiskey in and demanding to know where she was keeping us. He napped on the porch, limbs sloshed down the staircase like water flooding down the steps to the driveway. When he woke, the alcohol tempered to buzzed, he grabbed his keys and a bottle of Canadian Mist and started driving. Six days later he hazed his way up the highway, almost driving over the cliffs even though he never reached more than twenty miles an hour.

As he poured around the town, he growled out *Jackie*, accosting college students as they blazed on the lawn. Eleven months had passed since he'd seen his daughter. The rainy winter discharged Arcata slowly and his sneakers collected mud like a second skin, wrapping his feet in wet earth as he sludged toward the nearest shop.

Jackie heard him, watched his hobbled frame sway through the streets, like a broken down version of her brother, toward the windows at her work. Clutching his side, he repeatedly moved a hand to his coat pocket to check that the flask was still lodged in place. She ran to the back of the store, bricked herself in behind the fifty-pound bags of flour and salt. When he jolted into the café, skipping over the doormat and leaving mudprints around the tables, Jackie leaned around the shelves to glimpse him. His eyes registered hers but recognized only young woman, not daughter, and she dislodged herself and asked what she could get him.

"I don't want a goddamned coffee. Where's my Jackie? She's supposed to be here." He clumsied onto a chair and stared, waiting for her to bring out his child like a plate of food or a cappuccino.

JACKIE CALLED ME AN HOUR LATER, first words spoken to me in months and I recognized her voice at the initial inflection. Her father was still at the café, hunched onto a table, hand in his pocket with the flask half-visible. Gargling and passing in and out, mumbling her name even in his sleep. She was closing the shop alone and didn't know what to do. Call the police and let him end up drunk-tanked and released back to wander around searching for the daughter he didn't recognize even as he looked her over. Wake him up and reintroduce herself, allow him into the space she'd separated from her childhood world. Beg the guys over to load him into Bruce's truck and drop him emergency room curbside or sign him in as homeless and take off. She couldn't focus her thoughts long enough to decide and asked me to come help her fog through the options.

"Call Bruce, I'll bring Luke. Don't worry," I told her.

I explained Luke onto the street, justified helping Jackie. Her father was an intrusion, a recollection of all we'd abandoned. A dredging up of Iowa, of Danny. I wanted to keep my previous life from Luke, fall into who I was now as though I'd always been she, just waiting to escape and breathe. I zipped and unzipped my jacket, slid my feet without picking up, swallowed every few seconds until my mouth ran too dry to move my tongue. When I tried to slip my hand into Luke's, he scratched his nose and folded his arms across his chest, not even looking sideways. We'd been speaking in clipped phrases for weeks, addressing each other with practical questions and statements about needing more toilet paper, watering the orchid in the living room window, the forecast for the next day. Our tangling baffled me. We spoke more, affectioned more, engaged more when I was fucking other men. Now that I bedded every night at home, he barely looked at me.

Bruce met us at the café and nodded me through the door. Jackie stood behind the counter, one hand still resting on the phone by the register, the other's bony fingers curled around the handle of a coffee pot behind her. She startled when she saw me, looked to her father sleeping on the white-painted metal chair, scrolled flowers pressing into his back as he reclined, head angled back enough to jump his breaths out in halted gargles. I walked over and crouched by his side. When I shook his shoulder, he opened his eyes and blurted my name.

"Where's Jackie? You must know. You always knew."

"Jackie's right here, she's standing at the counter." I gestured over and Jackie small-flicked her wrist in a way that reminded me of the princess wave we used to practice when playing dress up in elementary school.

"My Jackie's a lot fatter than that girl. Don't try to trick me. I want to see my daughter."

Jackie's arm motioned itself to a cup, as though no longer part of her body, and poured coffee to just shy of overflowing. She walked around the counter edge slowly, shaking, frailing her way, suffering through each motion. I couldn't tell if she spilled the coffee on his lap intentionally or if her tremors made it impossible not to. Her father grabbed her wrist as she tried to set the cup on the table.

"Watch it, bitch!"

"Let go of my wrist, Dad."

He dropped his hand and lurched his way to standing, propped his elbow on the back of his chair for balance. Luke and Bruce moved closer, into grabbing distance of each of his arms, as he leaned forward to examine her eyes. Gazed up and down her frame, brow crunching at the sight of each angle he'd never before seen, each protrusion that used to be buried in muscle and fat.

"What did you do to yourself?"

"I remembered Danny. Looks like you seemed to forget him somewhere in the last hundred bottles of whiskey."

Bruce caught the arm just before it struck my cheek on the way to Jackie.

"Calm down, man. We don't want to call the cops. Just chill for a second, okay? Everything's cool," Luke said, securing his other arm.

"I ain't going to let my daughter talk to me that way. It's disrespectful."

"Look, no one's being disrespectful. We're just all a little tense. Let's just take a minute and breathe," Bruce said as he motioned Jackie back behind the counter. When I stayed frozen, Luke shifted his head toward the counter as he looked at me. I joined Jackie.

"We're gonna sit you down again, okay, dude?"

Jackie's dad continued to glare at her, but stopped struggling and relaxed into his chair. Bruce and Luke flanked him, dragged chairs to sit close enough to grab at his first flinch.

"What are you doing here, Dad? You shouldn't have come."

"I can do whatever I want, goddamn it!"

"I know, but you should have stayed in Iowa. There's nothing for you here," Jackie whispered at the floor, never looking at her father. Any trace of the man who cooked us burgers and taught us how to ride bikes had disappeared in the months we'd been gone. He slowly calmed down to bewildered, as though confused himself as to why he'd driven across country.

"I just, I wanted to..." He looked around at each of us. "I wanted to see my kid." He shook his head, chin dragging across his torn tee-shirt with an old company logo in red letters. "But you don't even look like my daughter anymore."

"And you look so much like my father," she snapped back.

Luke and Bruce stopped him when he stood and mumbled that he should leave, knowing he was too drunk to go anywhere and suspecting he had nowhere left to drive. We tried to convince a plan out of him, a report of what was going on back home and how he would continue his life, but all we could gather was a denial-laden accusation of people taking his job from him because his son had committed suicide. Jackie raised her hand but let it drop before she got close enough to strike him, the energy required, too much for her.

"Where will you stay?" she asked when he said he thought he'd remain in California.

"Dunno. I would have figured my daughter would be happy to put me up, but I can see you aren't exactly the girl I brought up anymore."

"You're not exactly that father, either."

"I'll camp somewhere."

"You don't know the area."

"Then I'll park my car and stay in there."

"The cops will ticket you and make you move."

"Fuck, Jackie. I don't know."

"Why don't you go home? Danny's dead, I don't want you here. Leave me alone and go back to Iowa."

They stared at each other, Jackie looking away first.

"I can't have you dredging up my old life, Dad. If you're going to stay, it's not with me, and I'm not going to be part of it. Take care of yourself, but leave me out of the process."

Jackie walked out of the store and across the street. I wondered who would shut down the coffee shop when we left.

"Hey, man, I actually need some help with landscaping. If you want to give me a hand with that, you can set up camp in my yard," Bruce offered. I stared at the croissants lining trays inside the pastry case, pulled at my fingers and looked back and forth between the door and Jackie's father.

"Thanks. I'd appreciate that."

"Alright, then, it's settled. Why don't you leave your car and get it in the morning? I'll give you a ride back to my place and we can get you set up. Luke, you guys wanna come over later and we can barbecue?"

"Sure. We'll pick up stuff to grill and some beer," Luke offered, despite my warning glare.

As Bruce drove off, Jackie appeared through the back door of the café and started pulling the day's pastries out of the case, wrapping semi-fresh cookies in plastic, moving cake slices and pudding cups to the refrigerator.

"Thank Bruce for me, okay Luke?"

"Of course."

He wrapped his arm around my waist and pulled me from the café to leave Jackie to close, before I could involve myself in worrying conversation with her.

"Give her space," he whispered as we walked toward the co-op.

We loaded our basket with spinach-and-feta chicken sausage, hot dog buns, green peppers, mushrooms, an onion, salt and black pepper kettle-cooked chips, and a twelve-pack of locally brewed beer. When I cried on our walk home, Luke shifted his bags to one hand so he could hold me. Jackie's father had passed out in his tent by the time we arrived and even the smell of the food didn't wake him. I accepted the joint Bruce passed, round after round, and fell asleep on the living room couch.

Jackie ignored her father as obviously as possible, flaunting her unwillingness to talk to him whenever she thought he would notice. She refused to visit him at Bruce's house, walked across the street at the first view of him on the sidewalk, passed over him in line when he came into the café for coffee. I tried to talk to her, following down the street at her side as she hobbled slowly toward her apartment, joints jumbling and creaking together, osteoporosis setting in before her twenties and hunching her back to question mark curled. She refused to acknowledge me until we reached her door.

"Stop trying to pretend you really think it's a good idea for my father and me to have a reunion. You just feel bad for the guy 'cause he's falling apart."

"I just don't want you to regret it later."

"All I am going to regret is not calling the cops instead of you when he showed up."

"That's not fair, Jackie. I didn't know what to do any more than you. You don't get to ask for my help and then get mad at me when you don't like my decision."

"He's my father. Not yours."

"What the hell does that mean?"

"You don't know what he was like, even before Danny died, and you didn't have to go home to him moping around drinking once Danny was gone. You didn't have to listen to him moan about how his only worthwhile child was now rotting in hell."

"I didn't know, Jack. You could have told me…" I didn't know how to offer sympathy for this, how to apologize for a shortcoming I didn't recognize I'd committed.

"What would I have said?" She turned her back and unlocked her door and I could see the XS tag sticking out of her organic cotton sweatshirt. From the way it hung on her, I would have guessed it a men's XL. "You can't come in. Go home."

"Don't just dismiss me. I promise I won't mention your dad again, just let me keep knowing you."

"I'll call you sometime soon. Maybe we can get crepes."

The door clicked and automatically locked behind the slouch of her moving up the stairs. By *get crepes* she meant go sit at the restaurant, drink black coffee, watch me eat. Pretend conversation until we got sick of looking at walls and utensils.

I TRIED TO IGNORE JACKIE'S FATHER, John, out of last grippings of loyalty. But part of me enjoyed feeling a tangible piece of family back in my life and I found myself joining the growers for get-togethers at Bruce's place. Jackie's father calmed into Arcata, relaxed into a lifestyle where he wasn't expected to abstain or support a notion of adult that no longer fit him. When I visited, he hugged his restraint into me, avoided asking about Jackie and instead passed me a joint or a beer and caught me up on the story someone was in the middle of telling.

"Luke's been talking about his life in Boston," John said as we hushed into the room. "Makes me glad I'm living out here." Luke and Bruce nodded my way as we sat down on giant pillows on the floor.

"So my last job, the one that finally drove me to come out here..."

"I thought that was frustration with college," I said.

"College would have been just bearable if I hadn't had to spend my weekends working at the most godawful pretentious champagne bar in the city. It was this super bougie place, walls all covered in avant garde aspiring art retro prints—"

"Can't artists do anything original? Right?" Dustin said.

"—with a mahogany base bar with the copper table tops, exposed brick walls and ductwork. The furniture was this mix—they called it 'eclectic' like they fucking coined the word—of old tables and overstuffed sofas reupholstered in a mix of 50s floral prints and flannel and bright colors everywhere. Weird lamps and hanging lights. Very high-end loft meets hipster bohemian."

"How ironic," Bruce laughed.

"Yeah, it was absurd. If the people who came in there weren't dead set on appearing cultured, they'd have taken one look around, laughed, and gone somewhere that wasn't trying so hard. But that was the thing, everyone wanted so badly to be *in* on the atmosphere, to understand it as if it were some weird brilliant piece of art hanging in MOMA."

I gulped a slosh of beer to keep from snickering. Luke was describing half the businesses in Arcata, the underlying attitude of so many growers. This sudden money wanting to be cultured, in the know. Half the stores in the city catered to the same compulsion.

"There was an open kitchen where the cooks made ridiculously tiny servings and called them small plates; charged way too much because they were being *innovative*, you know, using foams and sous vide cooked meats and an occasional liquid nitrogen preparation. People ate that shit up, just loved the adventure so much that they didn't realize they were getting only one or two bites but paying fifteen, twenty bucks per dish. I mean, the chefs were good, but it was no French Laundry, " Luke shook his head.

"Were you a chef then, or a bartender, or...?" I asked.

"I was the head bartender on the weekends. Every time I walked into the place, I wanted to burn it down. The customers, nice enough as many of them were, all wanted to prove themselves. I mean, a lot of them ordered champagne, and they, surprisingly, weren't too bad. Most people don't try to pretend to know a lot about champagne, or they just stick to the famous labels or ask for recommendations. The obnoxious ones were the customers who tried to engage in conversation about other wines. All thought they were fucking sommeliers.

'Do you have something that's fruit-forward but not going to ambush me with plumminess, you know, nothing too quaffable—it's got to be bold—and with a really velvety mouthfeel?'"

"Something jammy, undertones of leather and tobacco—" I said.

"Rounded out with the intangibles of a college athlete," Bruce quipped.

"You mean aggressive and robust?" joked Dustin.

"No, I meant more of a team-player, full of spirit." We all laughed and toasted with our microbrews. Not so different.

"Yeah, yeah, just like that. I mean, Jesus, just because you read wine labels doesn't make you a wine snob. Ugh, anyway. Needless to say, I felt like every time I went in there, I was selling my soul to some dark, food and beverage devil."

"How long did you work there?" asked Nick.

"Oh, I wasted my weekends in that hell hole for the better part of two years."

"Dude, I wouldn't have lasted a week," said John, sounding strangely natural with young slang. Each week he spent in Cali, the more like an older brother he felt to me.

"Yeah, well, for the last six months, it was all I could do to make it through each shift. The only way I did it, the only way I *could* do it, was to pretend that all the people who came in were escaping a great conflict outside. That we were their last refuge, their last chance at civilization. Every night, I had to put on this great show for them because, at any moment, the world would come crashing in to kill them, a la *Hotel Rwanda.* They were refugees enjoying a last moment of luxury at my establishment, and, goddamn it, at least I could give them that!"

"Dude, Dad was so pissed when you quit that job," Bruce teased. "He actually called me to see if I could talk you back into it and into finishing out school."

"Seriously? I thought you guys hadn't talked in a couple years. Well, you know, I am the favorite son," Luke sat tall and mock-puffed his chest, "he's got to make sure I'm well taken care of."

"Of course. I *am* my brother's keeper. Why would he call me to discuss my own life?" Bruce laughed, "but yeah, I told him to talk to you about it, knowing that neither he nor Mom would. You could have actually murdered those people at your work burned the building down and they would have hugged you and said they understood. Probably even would have helped you if you'd asked."

"*You're* the favorite?" I teased. "No way. I don't believe it. Bruce for sure."

"Nope, I can get away with whatever I want," Luke smiled. "Doesn't matter what I say to them, they never contradict me. It's a little weird, actually... But, like I'm going to turn that down."

"The flipside is they don't actually care if he does anything worthwhile," said Bruce. "He gets praised no matter what. No work ethic, this one."

Every time I heard Luke tell a story, surrounded by friends, I realized how little he talked to me at home, how little I actually knew him. We'd merged our lives but I was almost no part of his. I tried to imagine a few years forward, whether I would figure into any telling of his history or just get phased out with his parents. Bruce was a closer friend to me than Luke, and I wondered at the ability of two people to exist completely separately together.

We kept swapping stories into the night, but Luke was done revealing anything, acting only as a foil for Bruce's telling of cross-country adventures. They'd traveled together when they were younger, just the two of them, camping and hiking the Appalachian Trail, canoeing in Canada, crossing the border into Mexico for a few days of drunken shenanigans. I'd never had a sibling beyond Jackie and Danny, never had a true blood connection to counter myself against, to determine my place in a family in relation to the other. Would I have been the favorite? Was I now, even as an only child? I dozed off with my head on Luke's shoulder, close, but still no closer to him.

JOHN ADOPTED ME AS SURROGATE for Jackie when he realized she wouldn't waver in her resolve to ignore him. Part of me felt the uncomfortable offness of the situation—in reality, he thought of me as extended family, and only treated me as daughter because his own avoided him—but I didn't care. My initial fears that he would bring home back to me, carry Iowa across the country to my doorstep, subsided as I realized he wanted to forget the state as much as I did. Instead, I found he brought with him the only part I missed, the degree of familiarity, of groundedness, that I'd yet to cultivate in Humboldt. He was person-I'd-known-for-forever, a memory pillar to lean against when I grew lonely.

We took trips to the ocean, sat on the sand at the edge of the water, both still awed and humbled by the strength and stretch of the water. The ocean both coaxing us in and pushing us away. In front of an active body so massive we felt insignificant and, in feeling so, were freed to be whatever we ended up as. Knowing I was nothing in the scheme of the world meant I no longer had to be something big. Whatever I did would be enough.

Mostly we avoided talking, leaving our conversation to mundane comments about the weather or a job or the shells we picked up on our walk down. Sometimes he'd start a story about one of his kids or his wife and stop himself, shy away from the remembering. I wasn't sure if it was to spare me or himself.

"Do you remember the time you fell off the roof?" I asked him on a breezy beach day that seemed to assure any words would be swept away by the wind and dissolved into the air after speaking. I wanted to clear my hazy child brain of half-memories with the assurance that the awkwardness would blow away afterward.

"Not really, no. But maybe I got a concussion," John teased.

"Oh come on, you must remember. The moms were yelling at you from the patio because you'd taken us onto the roof again to watch fireworks. Remember all those fourth of Julys when we could see three different shows from neighboring towns?"

"Oh yeah. The sky was so clear out there. You could see for miles, when there was something to see. I thought I just took you kids up to watch stars when the women were gone, though. I'd forgotten about that year."

"The one year you decided to dodge their scolding and take us up there while they were home, you had to go and fall. They never let us do it again! We climbed through Jackie's window onto the roof above the porch and you hoisted us up onto the slant above."

"Danny'd gotten too big, though. I didn't expect him to

weigh so much. Lost my footing..." He stared straight ahead. "Must've been that. Just didn't plant my feet well enough."

His silence. Soon I regretted voicing the memory. After he fell, my mother yelled me down from the roof, took me home with Jackie and Danny while their parents argued loud enough for us to hear tones without words as we finished watching fireworks from our kitchen. As she fussed around us, reassuring the twins that their father was alright, she mumbled about him having too much to behave that way, to risk the kids.

"Too much what?" I'd asked.

"Fruit punch." And I'd spent years afterward avoiding any potentially risky activities—monkey bars, swimming pools, forts—after drinking Kool-Aid.

Now, as he sat, I wondered whether he remembered clearly or made up story parts to fill in the gaps. I stood and pulled him up by both hands. I wanted to hug him, to tell him Jackie really loved him, to promise things would work out, be okay, that we'd both find ourselves out here on the west coast. To pretend he was my father, thank him for being a great dad, let him know that I saw him that way. But I picked up an empty clam shell instead, turned the blue-purple iridescence over to the rough side, the scabby growth of outer shell, and ran my fingers over it until a sharp ridge cut my thumb and the blood stained. I dropped the shell and buried it in the sand beneath my bare feet.

April 30

Dearest,

My wedding is a week from tomorrow. Who knew you could still get butterflies when you are my age? But I am. Although the ceremony and reception will be small, just a few close friends and some of Mark's siblings, I feel as though I've still so much to do! Some ladies from the church offered to help out—make flower arrangements, put on a potluck—but I declined. Politely, of course. I just want this to be special, up to Mark's standards. You should see the dress I found!

I wanted to touch base, thought maybe your reply to my invitation got lost in the mail. Mark and I are still hoping you'll be here to share in our day. I went ahead and ordered a dress for you in the size you always wear, as I figured you couldn't have gained too much weight in this last year. It's light blue and I promise it doesn't have any puffy sleeves! Mark wanted me to tell you he would love to pay for your plane ticket to come home for the event, if you are concerned about the cost. I bet he would even fly you first class! I'm not sure how you survive out there, just working in a record shop. Do you have enough money, dear?

What else? Oh, Jackie's father disappeared one afternoon and hasn't been back since. I don't know why I should find that odd, considering the past few months, but somehow things feel different with their house completely empty. Especially since he had been around every day after he lost his job. Mostly he sat on the porch and sipped what he called his iced tea. I secretly suspect it was some sort of alcohol, but you know I don't like to gossip. A gentleman from the bank stopped by here the other day, mistook our house for his, tried to tell me if I didn't pay my mortgage they were going to have to force me out. I told him he best go check that he had the correct address because I own our house outright. He shuffled to his car and drove next door—I don't know why he didn't just walk!—and knocked for a good two and a half minutes before giving up. I don't think anyone will be back to that house.

I was feeling so bad about that poor family and all their loss that I visited Danny's grave last week. Funniest thing, there was parsley growing all over the top of his grave. A whole bunch of flowers and even a tomato plant had taken root nearby and were blooming just beautifully. Makes sense, you know. Remember the gardening I taught you kids when you were all little? (You hated it so much when I made the three of you stop running around and help me out!) You use companion plants like parsley to attract the wasps and flies so they'll protect the other plants, the single plant helps the whole garden flourish. Anyway, I know you don't like talking about Danny, so I imagine you don't like reading about his grave. How is Jackie dealing with everything? Is she still so skinny?

Let me know soon if you'd like Mark to arrange your flights. I imagine the tickets are getting more expensive every day. While I'm not trying to pressure you, do remember that I haven't seen you in nearly a year, I'm not getting any younger, and who knows when there will be another wedding in our lives?

Speaking of which, have you met any nice young men out there? I know I promised before not to pry, but I am so curious about what life is like for you. Ever since you were a little girl, I imagined you finding and marrying a handsome banker or maybe even an architect. Do you remember how you used to play dress up with Jackie? The two of you would take turns making Danny pretend to be the groom while you paraded down an invisible aisle in the living room. Sometimes I'd cut you flowers so you could pull petals for the flower basket. You were such beautiful little children.

I love you!
Mom

BRUCE CALLED LUKE when Jackie's father disappeared. He didn't know Jackie's phone number, but I knew that wouldn't have made a difference. Luke told me Bruce found his tent dismantled and rolled up on the porch, a note scribbled on a scrap of paper. He'd gone to the hospital, it hurt to breathe and he couldn't stop peeing. He thanked Bruce and asked him to tell Jackie he loved her and was sorry. The note ended with an apology for taking a couple beers from the fridge the other night when he'd run out of his own.

We arrived at the hospital before I could reach Jackie. Her cell phone was off, the café was closed on Mondays, and who knew where she went when she wandered around Arcata. I figured she was huddled in the redwoods, gnawing on bark when the hunger overcame her, spitting out slivers of wood like watermelon seeds. The fluorescent lights set off a headache stampeding through the front of my brain, hoofing more dread with each step toward a nurse or doctor who looked as though he might offer answers. I imagined being stuck here, tubed to a bed, letting medical students examine me as a test subject: can you diagnose what's wrong with this one? I liked to think I'd present an interesting case, something exotic, with an affliction they'd practically thank me for having so they could learn with real life experience.

When Luke whispered the news in my ear, I imagined the hospital food the nurses would bring me, their special specimen, on mauve plastic trays. Individual servings of jello—would I prefer red or green today?—and grey lidded plates of mashed potatoes scooped like ice cream next to a pile of previously frozen chicken nuggets. I'd ask for barbecue *and* sweet and sour sauce and they would bring me both, without question. *I'll have Sprite in a cup with no ice, thank you.* When Luke whispered it again, I collapsed backward into his arms, let myself fall as the fluorescent lights danced through my retinas. Luke sat me on a cheap sofa with wooden arms as Bruce ran to get a cup of ice water.

"I'm sorry," Luke said.

"Why? He wasn't my father," I mumbled as I dazed in and out of my headache. "Someone should tell Jackie."

"I think you should be the one to tell her. But we can think about that later."

"He used to let us climb onto the roof, even in the thunderstorms. Stood quietly while we laughed and raised our arms in the rain. He built us a tree fort." Jackie told me he wasn't my father, and she was right. But she was also wrong.

"He must've been a great guy. Hell, he fit right in with all of us..." Luke trailed off. His comments would be relegated to those of visitors—in-laws, cousins, co-workers' spouses—at a wake with no real connection to the body in the casket.

"I called him Pops, sometimes." The lights seemed to flicker every few seconds, flashing like old photograph bulbs with the subjects sitting straight-backed uncomfortable as the film developed. "What did he die of?"

"Alcohol-related liver disease. They think it had been going on for years."

"Before Danny died?"

"They said his liver looked like he'd been drinking heavily for at least a decade."

How would I rewrite my summers and sleepovers to include my best friends' father as an alcoholic? How had I spent years under his care and never known? I wondered when Jackie first knew, when she first realized his happiness or relaxation or anger was a byproduct of alcohol; whether Danny had known; how much of our lives, so shared, had been hidden. As I tried to resurface old memories I recognized the temptation was to too easily find examples. If I wanted to, I could guess that every overly affectionate moment, every extra burst of anger, every stumble or misstep was a sign. But, I couldn't know for sure, now. And I didn't want to rewrite our joint lives this way.

"I want to see him."

"Don't you think we should just go? Let's leave and find Jackie, tell her what happened. We can all come back later, together."

"I don't think I'll be able to believe this is real unless I see the body."

The doctors refused to allow us into the morgue, saying

we had no authorization because we weren't relatives. When I screamed insults at a doctor, tried to claw past him to the doors leading to the ER, he called security. Luke and Bruce carried me outside, my arms still wriggling and reaching.

"I FIGURED THAT WAS WHY HE CAME TO VISIT," Jackie said when I found her on a bench in the park. "He was making amends."

We sat together and I held my questions right below my voice box, wanting to loose them into sound but afraid of angering Jackie. I didn't want to be inappropriate. She pushed me sideways to make more room and settled her head on my lap.

"Sometimes I would ask my mom what my dad kept locked in his cabinet in the workshop. She'd get mad at me and tell me to mind my own business. Sometimes she'd start crying. I didn't understand. He was a functional drunk."

"I'm so sorry." I stroked her hair.

"No, it's okay. Life can be weird, it has a strange sense of justice. I think my mom wanted to leave him for years, but couldn't find an excuse to. The whole no divorce religious thing and all that. But after Danny died and my dad no longer tried to hide his drinking, I guess she finally felt validated to leave, at least in the public eye."

"But what about you?"

"Yeah, well. Danny was the favorite anyway." She saw my frown. "No, no, it's true. And it's okay. Besides, our mothers were as destructive to us as my father was to my mother, just in different emotional ways."

"I don't want to remember your dad as a drunk."

"Neither do I, so let's not."

"Jackie?"

"Yeah?"

"I'm worried about you."

"I know. But I've got it under control. Let's not talk about it, okay?"

We watched the sun drop over the buildings in town, crawling down through the fog over the corners and edges of the gas station, the grocery store, the overpriced clothing shop. Jackie didn't want to see her father's body and had told the hospital to cremate him and get rid of the ashes. Our only memorial to him was swapping our childhood over beers and weed later that evening, Jackie back for a single night, Bruce's house feeling almost unchanged from our arrival the previous summer.

L UKE AND I DROVE TO SAN FRANCISCO as spring edged through Arcata. His parents had flown across country to explore the city and visit wine country, and wanted to take us to dinner to meet their son's girlfriend. I didn't realize Luke had told them about me, as he seemed to keep his Humboldt life pretty private from people back east. Even though we lived together, I didn't know I figured prominently enough in his mind to warrant an introduction in his brief, irregular phone calls home.

Not wanting to make the six and a half hour drive back to Humboldt after dinner, we decided to make a weekend of the trip and booked a hotel room in the city. Bruce gave us a triple vacuum-sealed package to deliver to a customer, a smaller pack for his parents. When I asked Luke how they'd get the weed back home on their flight, he shrugged and said they'd been doing it ever since Bruce moved to California. Apparently, if you sealed it properly so the dogs wouldn't smell it, wrapped it in an empty box of cheese crackers or the such, and put it in with your luggage, it was unlikely to be flagged in the checked bags. I decided I would like his parents. My mother, even if she got over its illegality enough to smoke pot, would die of nerves before she even boarded a plane with her checked bag carrying the stuff.

San Francisco, chilly all year long, approached its winter weather as Arcata approached summer and a constant breeze made the air run goosebumps along my skin. We drove over the Golden Gate Bridge, the fog climbing up the columns so they appeared to us as giants rising from the mist as we approached, disappearing into the grey behind us just moments after we drove under their legs like kids playing freeze tag. The cables vanished upward into white haze, appearing to defy gravity and hang, ends suspended, reaching toward the sky. I'd never seen the bridge before, but years of hearing about how incredible the man-built structure is, tales from classmates who visited, and countless postcards and images in books set me up for a breath-stealing moment of beauty. But after watching Jackie diminish herself and a semi-father die of a disease I never knew he had, the bridge appeared as just another bridge, large and metal and cabled, connecting one side to another.

I watched out the window as Alcatraz appeared in the bay, the rock island jetting out of the ocean, a white metal water tower near a short long building windowed evenly. I thought I saw a lighthouse. A sailboat moved across the water in front of the island, appeared as tall as the cliffs that rose to reach the jail, and I imagined trying to escape the place, the ice of diving into the Pacific after making it past the guards. I couldn't remember if the stories I'd heard of Alcatraz ended successfully or with the prisoners being recaptured or killed.

Luke parked the car and checked our bags into the hotel in the early afternoon. We set out across the city on foot, with no plan except to reach the restaurant by the wharf by seven-thirty: an early dinner, by our northern, northern Cali standards. I bought a coat at the first clothing store we found, a too-expensive piece of mock-wool just enough to cut the wind, but didn't mind paying. What else would I do with the cash I'd put away from my life in Humboldt? My perception of price had made an upward swing after a year in the area. Tags I balked at before now seemed reasonable, even a bargain. We stopped for chocolate, soup and sourdough; ducked in galleries where we critiqued work we knew we could never create as if we'd painted three of better quality the day before; searched racks at record and clothing stores and indoor markets. At a small shop we discovered flowering teas: tiny packages of leaves that bloomed from dried to full flowers in the clear wine glasses the quiet young woman served up with scalding water. I stared at the blossoms, wondering how they could look so alive in water hot enough to wither them.

The restaurant overlooked the bay, but we sat indoors viewing the street instead, so we wouldn't shiver our way through the meal. Luke's mother hugged me the moment she saw me, hooked her arm through mine on our way to the table as if we'd been best friends for years. His father nodded and smiled at Luke an approval of my appearance, shook my hand firmly, pulled out both his wife's and my chairs before we sat. Ordered cocktails for the table, shut down the waiter's request for IDs before it even reached vocalization, requested a bottle of white be ready when the appetizers arrived, a red for the entrees. The parents made small talk—weather, location of family, jobs—while Luke's father chose several appetizers for the table.

When Luke's mother tried to order a glass of a different white, her husband cut her off and told the server just to bring the bottle he requested.

"She doesn't know what she's talking about," Luke's father said, expecting the server to agree with him. "We'll order the main course later, please," he waved away the server, then turned to me. "I do hope you like mussels. They'll go perfectly with the wine I've ordered. Not to worry if you don't, though, I got an array of starters for us. I know not everyone develops a taste for them right off the bat. You'll have to get Luke to take you down here more often, as I imagine there isn't much to speak of in the restaurant scene up north. We'll give you a list of recommendations."

"Honey, let her reply," said Luke's mother, though, by now, I was too afraid to say something wrong.

The few times Luke spoke of his parents, I couldn't understand his underlying frustration at being over-indulged. My mother never gave me extra, though provided plenty. I didn't have another sibling, so I couldn't tell if she spoiled me more than she would anyone else. But, whenever Luke complained about his parents treating him differently from Bruce, I got annoyed. Mostly, he laughed about being the favorite, but beneath his brushing it off, I sensed discomfort. A disdain for being appeased. After hearing his father speak to his mother, though, I wondered if the attitude of dismissal—the flick of the wrist to the server to shoo him away, the undermining his wife's ability to choose—applied unevenly to Luke and Bruce. Would being the golden child feel good if it came at the expense of others?

"I've never had mussels, but I'm sure I'll love them," I ventured. Luke's father nodded.

"Luke tells us you are thinking of enrolling in college in the fall. What do you plan to study?" His mother smiled, genuinely interested in a subject I had never discussed with Luke. Had he created an entire persona for me, a girl I was supposed to be for his parents, someone who would meet all their criteria? He avoided my eyes and brushed my squeezed hand off his leg. My lifestyle, my personality, all the reasons Luke supposedly loved me weren't enough now, and to his parents I had to be another, better, person.

"Yes, well, I haven't decided yet. I'm afraid my interests are too varied at this point. I'm debating between mathematics and biochemistry," I lied, reinventing myself again. Luke still wouldn't look at me. I wanted to turn to him, accuse him of setting goals for me just like his parents did for him. The same goals he hated when his parents pushed but then, when he failed to meet them, hated when his parents stopped pushing.

"That's wonderful!" said Luke's father. "We need more women in science. Maybe Luke could learn a thing or two from you."

"Actually, I've been trying to convince him to go back and finish up his degree, isn't that right, honey?" I knew as soon as I said it, I shouldn't have. Something about the dynamic at the table made me so uncomfortable I wanted to stir up Luke's anger, I wanted to jump right into the tension and embrace it.

Luke kicked me under the table and gulped at his martini. I took a sip of my French 75, to give myself time to think and occupy my mouth so I couldn't speak. I'd crossed a line with him. Invited his parents into an off-limits conversation.

"I like this girl already," declared both parents, in sit-com-ish unison. We all canned laughed, awkwardly sought stable conversation ground. I realized for all I'd explained about my mother, Luke had told me next to nothing significant about his parents aside from his own role in the family, so I had nothing specific to ask them, no interested questions to throw their way. They worked, both, making lots of money doing something Luke found utterly boring. They had a regular home and a vacation home on an island somewhere warm. They were supportive. I wondered if Luke viewed them with the same disdain he did the patrons of the wine bar, if he cringed every time his father took a sip from a fresh bottle pour and nodded *acceptable* at the server.

The appetizers and wine arrived, providing another oral occupation. I asked a vague question about work and set Luke's father off on a half-hour monologue about the financial industry that I couldn't follow, even for the few minutes I tried. He sounded like he was giving a pitch at a seminar. I imagined him standing on a makeshift platform, risers dragged to the front of a large conference room or hall, perhaps in a swanky hotel, no podium, decked out with microphones hooked to headset around his ears. Raising the crowd in a supportive, self-affirming chant of success, selling out the signed copies of his books. I knew if I were an attendee I would buy the book, the whole spiel, just to avoid looking like a failure.

When Luke's mother tried to add to the conversation, he shut her down immediately.

"Look, honey, you just don't understand the markets as well as you think you do," he looked at me, shook his head with a pitying smile, turned to Luke and nodded. "You know I'm right, son."

We sat awkwardly for a moment, though Luke's father didn't seem to notice. He continued on about work, how he was having a record year and thought his wife ought to quit her job at the school. The entrees arrived and I was grateful for something else to shove in my mouth to alleviate the need to respond.

"How's your brother doing, Luke?" asked his father.

"Why don't you call him, Dad, and ask him yourself?"

"Because he doesn't call back."

"Maybe that's 'cause you don't really want to know what's going on in his life. You could try actually giving a damn for once."

"Boys, come on now!" said his mother. "Men! What can you do with them?"

"Can't live with them…" I mumbled.

"I, for one, maintain that we most certainly can live without them!" she replied.

"Right, sweetheart. And who pays our bills?"

"I contribute," she said softly.

"Only in token."

Luke stood up, grabbed the small package of marijuana from his coat pocket and threw it across the table toward his father.

"There. Bruce says hello." He pulled my chair backwards, nearly tipping me off the side, and grabbed my arm. "Thanks for dinner."

I tried to mumble my own thank you, goodbye as we walked onto the sidewalk. Luke's father didn't look surprised, and his mother just stared blankly ahead. When I looked through the window once outside, they were already back to conversation, Luke's father motioning with his hands, threatening to spill their drinks, his mother nodding and taking tiny bites of her dinner.

"Seriously, Luke? I can't believe you just pulled me out of there like that! I am so embarrassed."

"What, you wanted to listen to my dad berate my mom about fucking money? That's all he ever does. He's an asshole. You're not the only one who can't stand to listen to your parents."

"At least I don't make up things about people I'm seeing so they appear up to snuff for my family!"

"At least I told them about you." He glared. "You just pretend I don't exist in your life. You're too scared to tell your mother you have sex, too scared to tell her you might actually be bisexual. You'll go your whole fucking life before

116

you stand up to her and tell her you disagree. Find your way back to Arcata, here's some cash for a flight. When you grow up, call me again."

He crumpled a few hundred dollar bills out of the folded wad in his pocket and threw them toward me. Some fluttered to the sidewalk, others stuck to my jacket, clenched there in the wind.

"You can't leave me here in the city, Luke. What about my bag at the hotel?"

"I'll bring it back with me at the end of the weekend."

"How will I get home? Please, I don't know San Francisco!"

"Neither do I. You'll figure it out. Ask a strange man for a ride, you're good at that. I bet you'll find a way to barter."

"That's not fair."

"You're one to talk about fair."

"Don't do this. I rode down with you."

"Just go home. Decide if I'm really your boyfriend or just your west coast secret fuck."

I hitchhiked back to Arcata, spent the whole ride in a contact high from the joints the young couple up front passed back and forth, and ended up covered in hair from the large mutt who draped across my lap. When I got home, I unlocked our apartment tentatively, trying to assert a claim to the space and our life together but unsure if it was valid. I pulled a bottle of red wine from the cabinet above our sink and a container of leftover curry from Japhy's from the fridge. The last sheet of Crane stationary sat on my side table and I grabbed it and started a letter to my mother, outlining the sins I had committed against her faith since I'd been in California. *Fornication, intoxication, blasphemy*. I explained Luke as *partner, boyfriend, roommate. Lover*. I would not be coming home for her wedding, but please thank Mark for his generous offer. Should I send a gift to the old address or would they be moving elsewhere? I spilled over both sides of the single sheet and when I realized I was writing down the table, I grabbed some college ruled loose-leaf from Luke's desk.

Words escaped onto the pages: *evolution, sex, drugs, atheist. I never read your Bible verses, so you may as well stop sending them. Jackie's father was an alcoholic and you never told me. He's dead. Danny and I dated and never told you. I intentionally miscarried, you would have been a grandmother*. Everything I wrote coming as a confession to incite ostracization. *Cut me out of your life, Mother, because I cannot cut you out of mine*.

I photocopied the letter and placed it in an envelope on Luke's pillow and mailed the original immediately, before the buzz courage of the wine and the fear of Luke leaving wore off. Days later, when he asked me to come home from camping in Bruce's yard, Luke thanked me and told me he was impressed that I had the courage to write all that. *But you didn't mention Jackie*, he said, and we patterned back into our stagnant pre-San Francisco selves.

A MANILA ENVELOPE ARRIVED IN THE MAIL for me with no return address. I slid my fingers under the extra layers of Scotch tape, bent up the flimsy metal tabs, slipped open the cover. Turned the opening to the table because I didn't want to reach inside. My mother's handwriting of my address: even though I could tell she tried to disguise it, the letters were too controlled to belong to another hand.

A half-page note spilled out, still written on stationary, still in beautiful lilting scrip but with the sentences interrupted, marred, by tiny drops of salt water. Words like *devastated* and *shocked* and *believe*; outlined ideas of daughter and the required behavior of such a position; promises to pray for me, of unconditional love. *I tried to raise you better than this.*

A smaller envelope fell out, sealed, which I opened to reveal a note in foreign handwriting, all lines that jammed into each other, jutted up to form modern architectural letters, the hard sentences of a man who thought he'd be a stepfather. Mark told me how cruel I was to send a letter such as that right before my mother's wedding day, how inconsiderate it was to them both. *You should be grateful to have a mother who can forgive, even if you never come around or apologize.* He included a check for three thousand dollars to help me find my own apartment so I would *no longer feel dependent on a man for housing.*

I stared at the enclosed photograph, a print sepia-toned intentionally, *to look timeless and elegant,* I could hear my mother say. Mark's tall, squishy stature next to my mother. Her delicate sheath curving loosely around her, shoulders modestly laced in slight off-white. A smile I recognized as settled, as secured into a new life without worry for money, only for clean house and dinners, for her wayward daughter. A teenager I didn't recognize wearing a dress of what I imagined to be light blue, two sizes too big, the one she ordered for me, Mark's unmentioned first marriage's child trying her best to fill out the outfit of a first choice who didn't show. The old farmhouse in the background, new beds of flowers around the porch, tulle wrapped around the railings and support posts. A bouquet of sunflowers, a single blossom overpowering the new husband's grey suit lapel.

A small Bible fell out, inscribed with my name on the cover, my mother's handwriting on the first page. *This is how you were raised. Don't turn your back on home.* A few sunflower petals fell from the pages as I tossed it across the room toward the closet.

I took Luke out to dinner. Told him about the letter, the Bible, the photograph. He didn't know how to be supportive; parented without the condition that he believe out of tradition and upbringing, he tried to offer jokes to lighten the story. I tore the check in half and mailed it to my mother with nothing else in the envelope. I wrote Mark a no-thank you note. Told him the two of them look lovely and happy and I hoped the reception was nice. Asked him to hug my mother for me.

The second time I missed my period, I scheduled an appointment for the following week at the local clinic. As I stared at the positive pregnancy test that prompted the call to the doctor, I couldn't imagine the words *I'm pregnant* ever leaving my lips again. At the initial consult, my doctor said I was already into the second trimester, that it was not uncommon for women to have periods during the first few months of a first pregnancy. I never corrected her. At home, I flushed unused tampons down the toilet so Luke would still see the purple plastic tubes wadded in toilet paper I tossed in the small basket under the sink. We never discussed our opinion of children beyond both stating we thought the world was overpopulated and that crying babies were a pain in the ass anyway. We never discussed our perspective on abortion. Luke didn't need to know. No one needed to know.

Each day that week I woke disoriented, my mind having flipped its way through so much worry overnight that I lost track of where I really was. Luke shook my shoulder, asked if I was okay.

"You were whimpering every few minutes," he concerned.

"Must have been a bad dream."

"Babe, you're covered in sweat. Do you remember what the dream was about?"

"Nope, no idea. Weird, huh?" I climbed out of bed. "Wanna grab breakfast out?"

Arcata never seemed so full of children and pregnant women. Hyper-tuned, all of a sudden noticing because I wanted the subject off my mind, I felt inundated by the images. Even pancakes made me think of my toddler days, my new friends Jackie and Danny sitting with me at our large farmhouse table as our mothers busied preparing for and cleaning up after us. I didn't want that, couldn't do that. I would make a horrible parent at nineteen and I knew it. My patience ran out with adults in grocery lines who didn't understand that Express Lane really did mean ten, not seventeen, items. My daily routine was selfish and I had no plans for where to go next. How could I learn to speak child and grow responsibility in less than a year?

Luke knew I was internally debating with myself and that he wouldn't be able to talk to me. If I told him, would he try to convince me to keep the baby? Would he believe it was his? I hadn't slept with another man in several months, but I'd ended up more than three months along without even knowing it. What if some drunken night... I blotted out the sensation memory of foreign fingers to keep from wanting someone else. Better not to revisit.

I imagined my mother in the simple wedding dress she'd worn a month before, thought of her old station wagon with the pro-life and Christian fish bumper stickers, heard her chastising of the television for stories of abortions tinning through my ears. Miles away from the Quad Cities, I still felt close enough that her anger could leave a welt across my wrist. Or maybe her disappointment. If she knew, she would rail against my going through with the appointment, accost me for even considering it. And when I acquiesced, she would berate me for conceiving in the first place and question when I was planning on marrying the father. Even a middle ground felt more welcome than the extremes of motherhood, but I saw none.

TWO NIGHTS BEFORE MY APPOINTMENT, my stomach cramped. I doubled to the bathroom, listing my dinner and my lunch in my head, thinking maybe it was food poisoning. Too late for allergic reactions. Huffed myself to sitting at the edge of the tub, slumped down to the floor as the blood sobbed out of me. Luke ran at my scream, hooked himself under my body and rocked back and forth as I pressed and discarded fresh toilet paper against myself to catch bright red clumps of tissue, over and over in a daze. Curled and pressed to his chest, I fingernailed into his arm, wailed with the last of my voice as the blood began to subside. Splotched red repainted the white tiled floor with an abstract mural of something unwanted, now mourned when taken unwillingly.

Luke lifted me into the tub, stripped off the stained panties that had fallen to my ankles, pulled off my crepe-light tank top and ran the shower over my head. Cleaned up the strewn toilet paper, carried the bag downstairs and into the trashcan perched streetside so it would disappear with the morning trash run. He'd just found out about the pregnancy but pretended he'd known all along, shushed my crying with kisses against my forehead, climbed in the tub fully-clothed, and cradled against me. When he tried to move me to the bedroom I refused. He built a cushion of towels beneath us, grabbed a lime green throw blanket from the living room, removed his soaked shirt. His hands caressed me lovingly, without desire, and I fell asleep to his fingers over my neck and scalp, dreaming of parsley and wondering whether a single leaf from sprigs a year before had taken root and grown inside me.

We spent a month determining ourselves against each other. Days tripping into my fault, your fault, no fault. Luke hid whatever anger he felt over my excluding him from the pregnancy decision behind his concern for me, but the choking back of accusations was visible as his face contorted in conversations about grief. *You were going to abort it anyway*, I imagined him accusing. *Why should you be so sad now?* I didn't know how to explain the sorrow, the way I felt both a distinct loss and a sense of relief. I wrestled with my guilt, not over the planned abortion, but over the distance I maintained from Luke, that I had from the first moments of our knowing each other. We had grown, but never close. How long could we call a friendship with occasional sex a committed relationship? Should we?

I thought of calling Jackie, begging myself to her apartment to cry, but I feared I would mention Danny and years of a hidden miscarriage. Our still-shared connection was tentative enough that I didn't want to risk it, so I buried myself into bed and work at the record shop. Luke told Bruce about the miscarriage, escaped out of our apartment to work through things in the company of family. I wondered whether he called his parents, told them they'd lost a grandchild. If he had, he would have spun a story around it, glorified it to the appropriate level of commitment and sorrow for them. My bitterness acted as a salve and even as I closed over, a wound trying to repair itself, I slathered it over and over, reapplying layers of sarcastic thoughts and snide comments of Luke across my mind.

THE FIRST FINGERS ACROSS MY STOMACH and under my
pants registered only flickers of the thrill I expected.
He came into the record store right before closing,
flipped through indie albums and asked my opinion. Flirted as
he listened to track after track, bought every disc I recommend-
ed. Passed me his phone number with the cash for the CDs.

Luke was gone, a quick-scribbled note—*love you, call me
at Bruce's if you need me, see you tomorrow*—cornered beneath a take-out carton of deli-prepared couscous salad and
roasted Brussels sprouts on the kitchen table. Jackie's voice
on the answering machine asked me for coffee in the morning. I'd already watched all our DVDs.

Matthew answered on the second ring without the usual
questioning tone people take when they don't recognize the
number. Responded to my tentative *hello, we met in the
record store earlier* with *I know.* He took me for dinner up
the coast, far enough out of town that I felt sure of avoiding
people who would recognize me. We had nothing in common
but lust, our conversation lulling forward with euphemisms,
subcontexting every mundane statement. He was unabashed-

ly physical, unconcerned about making the other diners blush, continuing to rub too high on my leg as the waiter spilled while refilling our water glasses. I didn't care, my mind racing through the dinner to imagining his apartment, the flash out of clothes, the climb through the space still dark from rushing without turning on lights. Matthew paid as I whirled through the last bites of my meal and we drove toward his place in complete silence.

The motions should have thrilled me, the unconstrained levering of ourselves over each other, crawling up and down parts I categorized through my head in Latin not English, new motionings and contortions. But I felt oddly unfulfilled, bobbling around him knowing a few hours later I would be searching for another set of parts to jut over and through me. When he walked to the bathroom to flush the condoms, I clothed quickly and grabbed my bag, zipping my fly as I ran down his stairs. He wouldn't be angry, I knew, and would probably call me some other weekend when he needed a second set of hands. Anatomy the only difference between us.

THE ONE TIME TURNED INTO THREE, then seven, then enough for Luke to pretend he'd just discovered the first. When I arrived home after work one afternoon, already planning to meet up with a man I'd seen a week before, my backpack was stuffed with clothes and a couple of books. Luke sat on the sofa, in the same spot as the first time he confronted me but without a beer in hand and with Bruce at his side.

"We think you should go to the hospital," Bruce said.

"That's an odd way to say hello," I retorted.

"Look, we didn't mean to ambush you, but we didn't even know when you'd be home," said Bruce. "You've been out all night, again."

"You know I love you Bruce, but this isn't your business."

"Like hell it's not," he replied. "You've stayed at my house, worked for me, vacationed with me. You're dating my brother but not even considering how your behavior affects him. How he comes to my house for support, to talk about how to stay in a relationship with a woman who cheats on him daily. When I see you self-destruct, see you needing help, I get to say something."

"Funny, you won't let me do the same for Jackie."

"This isn't about her. This is about you."

"I'm fine. All I need is space."

"You're fucking new men every night, running around not sleeping and then crashing all day in bed. Is that what you mean by space? Jesus. You need to get some help and figure this out."

"I don't need a hospital to do that. Luke, seriously, tell Bruce he's wrong. That he doesn't understand. That we're dealing with this our own way."

"I told you, you were breaking me," Luke whispered. "You've finished the job. Go to the hospital, deal with the grief. Decide what you want."

He walked out, slumped toward our bedroom. Bruce wrapped an arm around me, brotherish even when I hurt his real sibling, told me he'd visit and they'd probably only keep me a few days while they figured out some sort of medicine.

"You've been through a lot," he said. "It's okay to need help fixing it."

"What about Luke?"

"He's tough. He'll be fine, move forward."

"He won't be here when I get out, will he?"

Bruce didn't answer. He drove me to the hospital in his truck, sat with me in a small room that resembled a jail's holding cell more than a treatment room in a medical facility, hugged me goodbye, and passed my backpack to the nurse who guided me upstairs to the psych ward. They strip-searched me and handed me a pair of scrubs, promising me my own clothes once they inspected them for sharps and strings.

After a day of sitting in hard chairs signing forms, I craved sleep for the first time in weeks. Even if a man presented himself to me with doctor-stamped approval, I would turn him away for any more than a backrub. But after an hour of tossing, afternoon replaying in my head, I corridored the ward, counting my steps up and back down each hall until dawn.

WALLS IN HOSPITALS ARE PAINTED mock-happiness green. I imagine an obscure study indicated the color the most soothing and an enterprising company found its niche, supplying the standard hue of psychiatric wards in matte, semi-gloss, and high-gloss. The beds covered with scratchy low-thread count sheets stamped with *Property of* but no name. The psych tech brought more folded threadbare blankets, draped them over my feet, but I still shivered.

Mania—unearthed and dropped into a world of plastic silverware, paintings and photographs of flowers and buildings, schedules for the unscheduled hours—feeds into itself. The hospital was an imitation of life outside with a too-florescent eerieness, a too-practiced normality. Pace the hallway, past the bedroom where a man sits tapping his knee in sets of four, past the common area where the incessant soap opera incites an argument about political agendas, past the nurses' station where a bored twenty-something in pink scrubs reads *US Weekly*; pace the hallway long enough and a psychiatrist asks you to sit with him and discuss your agitation. Read, talk, move, breathe too much and they add another day. Life in a microcosm breeds preemptive-paranoia.

I spent the first two days pacing. Weeks before of sleepless nights, fingers tripping over skin, squirming under men large, men small, breath in ears, tied or loose tongues running paths down my skeleton borders, whisper, scream, all to escape the eight extra hours a day, never exhausted. But boredom accompanied by lithium-filled tiny paper cups that looked like they'd been stolen from the McDonald's ketchup line delivered me listless. On the seventh day, I rested. Plaid windows, little lines of wire strung through the glass, and reinforced set boundaries of constant closed-off airflow and fifteen minute open-door checks.

Danny visited me at the moment dusk takes over, collected shadows in cages and unhinged the trap door all at once so the grey spilled over itself to reach further into each corner. He perched on the windowsill and I noticed the roots of the parsley had reached his eyes, shot their way through the whites like the brown veins of dried blood.

"We could have gone west," he whispered and drew outlines of Redwoods on the wall, shadow-puppetted birds flying toward the invisible trees. "The three of us and no one would have known."

Honor your father and mother. Honor begets obey begets blind faith begets paralysis. Northern California, a land elevated to escape plan, miles of trees older than all our years combined and a fog that crept across states to envelop us. I stroked Danny's hand and watched wisps of thick air rise off his skin like liquid nitrogen. Jackie needs to hear what we are post-planning, grab her brother's other hand so she knows his pulse beats in synapses as my brain recreates our family.

"Where's Jackie?" I asked Danny but his hands had become insects on the walls, earthworm fingers climbing toward the ceiling.

He returned to soil and lay still for earth to wash over his empty skin, lungs, skull. In dusk, Danny climbs free from the box I helped lower and covers me with the extra blankets. Ghosts do not exist in the lessons of my childhood. The dead go to glory or torture. An eternity of my brain running its circles seems like punishment, whether in worship or agony. I sometimes still pray in the half-conscious way of automatic reverting; conversation with an omniscient specter I know exists only in the electricity of my brain but appears as three men to control my life. I would trade days of eternity for the déjà vu of fingers through Danny's black hair, which is Jackie's black hair, coarse strands tangled. A red sweatshirt pressed up against my nose smells of weed and vegetable oil; my back arches. Back in the hospital, green grew up the walls with the sun and Danny dissolved with the lithium in tiny paper cups.

THE DOCTORS DIAGNOSED A NERVOUS BREAKDOWN, attributed both mania and depression to stressors and loss, prescribed six pills a day. Twice a week I met with a counselor who tried to coax out the topics I refused to discuss. When I spoke, I wove stories of neglect and abuse, covering myself in false

blankets she could unravel, figuring once she felt I acknowledged my issues, I'd be allowed to leave.

"Next time, why don't we talk about your life?" she said
at the end of each session, and I stayed on the locked ward
for another few days.

I distanced myself from the colony of coded braceleted patients, ate my food in the corner of the kitchen, setting my
chair as far from the others as possible. During group meetings I walled myself to the side of the door or a double-pane
wired window. I refused to speak.

Lindsay, my roommate, slipper-socked back and forth
across our room, tapping the edge of her bed four times at
even intervals, shuffling over to tap the edge of mine three.
Raising watched wrist to line of vision every thirty seconds,
she broke into rhyme whenever the digital displayed a six. I
asked her why. She said she had to protect her mother. Stepping on cracks is only one way to hurt your parents. She
didn't want to be a bad daughter. When her father visited, I
left the room, not out of respect but discomfort. The first time
I met him, he moved to my bed, sitting close enough for me to
feel touched even without contact.

"You shouldn't be in here," he told me. "You're too young,
too pretty. How old are you? Check yourself out. I'll give you a
ride wherever you need to go." I clawed his hand off my thigh
and left just as Lindsay stepped out of our shared bathroom.

"Did you meet my dad?" she called after me as she first-
tapped her bed.

THE AFTERNOONS GLAZED AWAY IN FRONT OF ME, my eyes too tired and shifting to focus on any one movement. Patterned down into wake, sleep, medicine, I wore myself away in memories of Jackie and Danny, in pieces of auto-cognitive morphine that sent me off to catatonia. The space I'd occupied by running from Luke to other beds, I now filled with running from the day to short apparitions of myself wrapped in Jackie's arms. I imagined Jackie and Danny dancing together in their parents' beige carpeted living room on a Saturday night. Ten lanky years old, boom box dialed into the classical station that played disco for three hours on the weekends. Hands clasped, fingers straining to remain locked as they flipped around each other, back to back, spin to front, release to fingerpoint the ceiling. Jackie in cutoff jean shorts, pink t-shirt tied in a knot at mid-belly, Danny in one of his father's button-down shirts half open and an old pair of corduroys, me couched and laughing. Every time I tried to join them, the image dissolved like lithium and left my body charged but empty.

THE COUNSELOR ASKED ME WHY I thought I ended up in the hospital and I sarcasticked her a barrage of non-answers. When she told me I would sit in front of her every day for an hour, even if I chose not to answer, I threw the nearest object I could find—a hardcover self-help book jacketed in bright yellows and greens—as close to her temple as I could be sure would actually miss her head. She laughed and told me she'd been hit with worse, but could always have a couple of psych techs sit in on the sessions with us if I'd prefer. Or, I could just tell her what's going on.

"Can people grow plants inside themselves?" I asked.

"You mean, like if you swallow a watermelon seed will it grow in your stomach? No, I don't believe so."

"If you absorb a chemical from a plant, can it linger in your blood for years?"

"Well, I mean. I'm not a biologist, you know."

"But you must have studied some science, if you have a degree in psychology, right?"

"Of course, but… Well, my impression would be that no, that would not happen. Unless it were a psychotropic plant, then it might be possible for it to cause hallucinatory flashbacks for years. We can check with the nurses, they can look it up on their computer. Why? Have you taken any drugs? Mescaline?"

"No. How can I determine how responsible I am for the destruction of my boyfriend's, well, maybe ex-boyfriend's, faith in relationships?"

"Everyone is responsible for his own feelings and how he chooses to perceive the actions of others."

"That's bullshit. What if someone does something so horrible you couldn't even talk about it?"

"You'd still be the one who gets to decide how you respond."

"Have you ever sworn in front of your parents?"

"Yes."

"Did they mind?"

"They curse quite frequently themselves, so no, I imagine they didn't."

"Well, have you ever done something so wrong in their eyes that they sent you a goodbye letter?"

She nodded, not because she had wronged her parents in such a way, but because she felt as though she'd uncovered the source of my breakdown. She carefully wrote a few notes on her legal pad, drew a circle around one sentence. Seemed to place a little star next to another.

"Some parents don't know how to deal with children who don't fulfill the image they've built up for them since birth. This doesn't make either party wrong, it just makes the relationship more difficult to navigate, especially if the parent is reluctant to allow the child to develop her own perspectives."

"Do you have any children?"

A FIGHT BROKE OUT IN THE COMMUNITY ROOM late at night between Lindsay and a young anorectic who hoarded food in napkins and buried them under her mattress. The psych techs discovered her behavior when one of the men in the room across from her complained of a rotten smell in the hallway. They found six pieces of bacon, toast, a chicken sandwich, broccoli, a small handful of scrambled eggs and an indistinguishable mass of chewed and spit out food. She accused Lindsay of stealing a half peanut butter cookie she'd been saving and raked fingers across any exposed skin she could find.

"Fuck off! I didn't take your goddamned food," screamed Lindsay.

"Bitch! I know you took it for your daddy. Gotta keep him happy so he won't fuck you!"

Two large psych techs ran in just as Lindsay threw an elbow to the anorectic's cheekbone, which had landed by Lindsay's ribcage during an attempted tackle. The crack echoed even outside the tiny room, into the hallway where I had hidden myself against a wall. I watched one man restrain Lindsay as the other tripped toward the nurse's station, yelling for them to call a doctor. There was no need to restrain the anorectic. She lay on the floor half-propped against a plastic-covered burnt orange couch, blood dribbling out her nose, over into the pronounced ridge of her lips, into the hollow space by her collarbone. The doctor ordered her to the ICU and she never returned. Lindsay was locked in a seclusion room and returned to our shared space, sedated.

AFTER THREE WEEKS OF TREATMENT, the recreation therapist called me into a room to face the lead psychiatrist, two nurses and my counselor. Chaired in a semi-circle with an empty seat centered in the room and facing them, the group resembled a dissertation panel, ready to ask me to defend claims made and theories purported.

"We've asked you here for an intervention of sorts," said the psychiatrist.

"What the hell was hospitalization, then?" I retorted.

"Remarks like that speak to your unwillingness to get better. You need to participate in your recovery. Effective immediately, we will be increasing your dose of Zoloft, which the nurses will go over with you." The psychiatrist looked straight on as he spoke, while the nurses eye-darted around the room.

"I'd like to meet with you more often, also," added the counselor, smiling as though telling me I'd just won a lifetime supply of chocolate. "We're going to begin cognitive behavioral therapy, see if we can't address some of the negative thoughts you're experiencing by retraining the way you think."

I told them to fuck off when they asked me if I had anything to add and slouched my way out of the office and up the hall. I slipped into the small room housing a television and two bookshelves tiled with old self-help books. The walls were muraled with white roll paper markered up by a decade of patients copying affirmations from book to sheet, reclaiming the words. I hooked my feet over one arm of a sofa, bridged myself across the couch on my stomach. Rested arms on the side table, buried face into cushion without concern for germs. They lysoled the plastic coverings every day. I gripped, grabbed, tried to pull myself to grow another inch. Suddenly, being taller felt paramount, the secret I'd missed. I imagined stretching myself enough to encapsulate the apparitions that crowded my mind. Jackie had it all wrong, trying to disappear when she needed to grow.

A psych tech found me on his rounds twenty minutes later and asked me what I was doing. I gasped out my plan into the pillow, my lungs unable to capture enough air with my arms pulled so far in front of me. He shook his head, left to return with a nurse carrying a small cup of pills in one hand, a needle in the other. She tried to coax my hands off the table, unwedge my feet from the end of the sofa, but I dug in at each end like a giant staple holding the couch together.

"You can take this medicine, or I will give you a shot of it in your arm. It's your choice."

I was sick of non-choices. Medicine or medicine: the only choice, the delivery system.

"I'm allergic to sedatives." I lied. "Just let me finish growing."

She stuck the needle in my arm and waited for my grip to loosen. They hobbled me back to my room, arms ribcage tucked, my feet slipslopping over the linoleum. When I woke groggy and sore twelve hours later, I was certain I'd shrunk.

THE ONLY NON-FLORESCENT LIGHT IN THE WARD hung above the dining room table, in direct sight of the nurses' station. It swayed despite the stagnance of the halls, small circle tracing, a perpetual motion machine. The staleness of the air inside made smells more pronounced, heightened two day dirty hair to weeks of unwashed skin. I never realized dandruff had an odor. When I explained this to the nurses, they conferenced into their station but left the door open enough for me to hear them debating. Was this an olfactory hallucination or a side effect of higher doses of medication? I backboarded myself against the wall and slid down to sitting. The smell of the overcooked breaded chicken patties reached me before the meal cart was even off of the elevator and I leaned over, nauseous from the overwhelming odor of preservatives.

M Y COUNSELOR DRESSED AS IF HEADING TO COURT to defend a client: black pencil skirted, black pantyhose and kitten-heels, white buttoned shirt carefully tucked with a smart blazer she kept as a cape over her leather chair. Even the psychiatrist didn't have a leather chair, so I figured she brought it with her when she started at the hospital, some remnant of the image she'd conjured in her mind of an office after grad school, an important position treating the psychiatrically disabled among us at $125 an hour. Her diplomas, two, and certifications, four, hung glassed-over in frames behind the sofa where I sat. Her patients had to swivel to see the awards that she faced during each session.

"Let's talk about disappointment," she instructed me.

"Are you frustrated that your career isn't more glamorous?" I retorted.

"This isn't about me."

"You are me if I'd stayed in Iowa. We're not different enough to make you comfortable."

She shifted in her chair, chewed her black pen cap, flipped through the papers in the manila folder on her lap without looking.

"I bet you thought you'd have your own practice by now," I continued. "But instead you're stuck in a hospital where the patients are mostly untreatable. You can't talk someone out of schizophrenia, right?"

"Let's explore what makes you feel the need to lash out at others instead of confronting your own insecurities," she shifted.

"Why do you find it important for me to acknowledge some great disappointment? Doesn't your grad schooling allow people to be happy at underachieving?"

She stared at me, cockheaded, single eyebrow raised. Jotted notes on a random paper, the first time she used her pen for anything but a chew toy. We spent the rest of the hour alternating between middle schoolish staring contests and eye wanderings around the small room. At the end of the session, she handed me a side-stapled thick packet without a title.

"I'd like you to read through this for next time. It's about cognitive behavioral therapy. Changing your negative thought patterns. Your excuse for not going to college is that you learn better by reading than lecture, so here you go. Prove it. See you tomorrow."

I laughed at her, snided a remark about professionalism, and wandered up the hall to find some of the vanilla instant pudding whose scent had wafted under the door and past her white noise machine to tease me during the past hour.

We repeated our routine daily for a week. Fell into bantered insults as questions. She wanted to explore my whole history, feeling as though she'd uncovered a deep-rooted problem in our first meeting, but I wanted to forget it. The miscarriage, Jackie's father, and Jackie's slow suicide brought me here, but I was far enough away now. I knew they couldn't keep me here involuntarily.

Part of me wanted to stay. Comforted into my bed each night with a handful of pill shot chemical cocktails, I slept and woke to the same routine. My activities were as scripted as my meds. I was allowed, encouraged, to feel and dwell in my insecurities and fears. Of course, I was supposed to overcome them. But the longer I didn't, the longer I stayed false-worlded and secure. I began making up afflictions and phobias, new revelations of why I shouldn't be returned. When the staff took groups outside, I stayed in, not wanting to remember fresh air, not wanting nostalgia and smells that might entice me out. I refused visitors—Luke, Bruce, even Jackie—and signed a form preventing them from even calling, so I never knew whether anyone wanted to see me. Instead, I camped in my bed, visioning them on my ceiling. They said what I wanted while flickering in half-shadows across the walls.

I imagined leaving the hospital, deposited by bus at the edge of Eureka or Arcata, maybe a few bucks in my pocket and a bag, with my belt, shoelaces, and strings from my sweatshirts in hand, as though I'd just done time in prison. Each week I'd have to check in with a parole officer. Maybe find a job where they didn't discriminate against inmates. I wanted to keep the blue scrubs they'd dressed me in, as souvenir, potential Halloween costume, proof I'd been inside and survived.

I had cash buried in a small waterproof safe on Bruce's

property. He let me keep it there for a small monthly charge, even after Luke and I started having troubles. Perhaps I'd take off for Europe, join the ranks of expatriates. Maybe see another ocean. With too much possibility ahead, I began tapping like Lindsay, wishing I could ask her when she started and if she thought she'd ever stop. But she was too drugged after the incident, kept in a low state of functioning, able to raise spoon to lips to eat her oatmeal but her face never registering taste, good or bad. She snored into sleep by seven-thirty most nights, after dinner and before the final community meeting. The psych techs stopped insisting she come to the meetings, and even guided her to bed beforehand so she wouldn't interrupt with her lolling head and drool that needed wiping. Her father stopped visiting.

I CHECKED MYSELF OUT OF THE HOSPITAL on a Thursday afternoon, officially against medical advice. Psychiatrist, counselor, nurses all insisted I was leaving half of the work undone—*You've made so much progress, but there's still lots of room to grow!*—but I was at least stable enough that they couldn't keep me against my will. If I stayed now, I would hesitate to leave later, convince myself into dependency on the system and lose any sense of independence in the outside.

Armed with prescriptions and my backpack full of clothes, I called a cab and rode back to Arcata, picking at the peeling vinyl seat, looking through the dirty plexiglass at the back of the driver's head. I tipped him too much and got out a few blocks from the Plaza, determining whether the city looked different under the new haze of anti-depressants and mood-stabilizers, the sleeping pill-imparted good night's rest. But Arcata unfolded the same: shops for expendable cash, students writing essays longhand on blankets in the square, the smell of weed on passersby, everyone underdressed and so *chill*. I stopped to grab a sandwich and asked for a suggestion. The counter guy pointed out several that were *crucial*. He wrapped up both for me and I mind-planned a picnic with Luke at home to figure things out.

The apartment was packed, boxed neatly, my things on one half of the living room, Luke's on the other. The furniture remained in place, I imagined so we could go through together and choose who kept which pieces. Luke handed me a list of apartments he'd looked at that he thought I would like. He was going to live with Bruce for a few months while he figured out what he wanted to do. He'd already given the landlord our month's notice, leaving me with a week to move out.

When I apologized, he shook his head and grabbed a box to bring downstairs. The moving truck was due in fifteen minutes. I was wrong about the furniture, he planned on bringing it all with him.

"This should be enough to cover your half," he said as he tossed a small pile of hundreds on the table before grabbing a second box. I picked up another box and followed him down and back up the stairs, waiting for him to talk to me—chastise, yell, cry, whimper, anything—but he remained silent.

After the last of the boxes, I blocked the top of the steps

with my body. Tried to hug him, to kiss his cheek or grasp his
hand one last time, but he contortioned away from my arms,
around and down the stairs.

"I can't," he called up. "Take care of yourself."

L UKE KNEW MY TASTES. All those months when I was running around, avoiding learning about him, he'd paid attention to the details I never said, the small things that settled me into a space. Each of the apartments he'd written on the slip matched my idea of a good living space, but I settled on a second-story studio a few blocks from the Plaza. The place was more of a large loft than single room as the ad implied, with exposed beams and ductwork running the length, a kitchen set off with a gas range I'd never use but knew enough to admire, and space for a couch and chair separate from the inexpensive futon I purchased from a local furniture store. I took a few days off of work at the record shop, decorated the walls with cheap funky art from Target and more expensive pieces from stores around the Plaza. With carte blanche from the landlord to update, I brushed a large square of black chalkboard paint on the kitchen wall and kept a bucket of chalk in various colors on a small table nearby. I wired speakers for music around the apartment but refused to buy a television.

I overboarded it with the place, but it was the first dwelling that had been entirely mine, for which no one shared responsibility. No one could dictate my decorations, my style of furniture, the color of curtains I hung in the windows, the mat I put on the floor in front of the tub. I patterned my bed with bright circle sheets and building blocks of pillows. I blew enough money on kitchen supplies, cookbooks, pots and pans and a rack to hang them from the ceiling that I nearly regretted it. Almost-panicked, I called a few growers and asked for extra trimming work. Eventually, I justified it as an investment in learning to cook for myself, the cost of self-improvement. Mostly, I liked the look of the stark black metal rods and the chains dangling pots against the ducts that snaked along the ceiling. I stopped feeling the need to report to anyone, including myself, why I wanted something.

Luke stayed distanced to the outskirts of Arcata and Bruce's house. When I ran into him downtown he mumbled about needing more space; when I tried to catch his eye across the street he feigned interest in the shop windows. Bruce called occasionally to check in, see how I was holding up, pretended Luke and I were still talking but just too busy to reconnect. He updated me on his brother, a courtesy I thanked him for repeatedly despite his insistence that he was just telling me about his own life which happened to include a brother living in his house.

An envelope arrived in the mail with brochures from several universities with good mathematics and science programs and a note from Luke's parents saying they were sorry we didn't get to say proper goodbyes before but they'd love to see me again and I should feel free to name drop them to the admissions officers at any of these schools as they had been involved with all and knew the deans personally. The idea of college had escaped me for the better part of a year, but I turned it over in my mind and considered the possibility. No mathematics, certainly, but perhaps a liberal arts education would be a good next step? I wrote them a thank you note, asked them to keep in touch, and sent it along with a photograph from Luke's party months before.

Jackie agreed to come over, late enough in the evening that she wouldn't have to make excuses around the food, to see my new place and catch up. She oohed and ahhed appropriately over my decorations, knowing exactly which choices—the blackboard, the pot rack, the ultra-cool lamp snaked over my reading chair—she should most appreciate.

"You might never get rid of me, now!" she said as she flopped onto the chaise next to an oversized bookshelf I still needed to fill.

"Damn! You figured out my plan!"

She smiled and I felt familiarity even though the body before me was thin to the point of alien. Our rules already set, I couldn't question her about her health. In turn, she avoided asking me about the hospital.

We turned on music from our junior high years and danced in our underwear around the living room, finally collapsing across the frenetic pattern covering the hardwood.

"I think this rug could cause seizures," said Jackie.

"I should probably hang a warning sign on the door."

"Enter at your own risk: epilepsy-inducing rugs, over-stuffed sofas, inappropriate chalkboard drawings."

"I'll be bombarded. Everyone will be here, all the time."

"Would that be so bad?"

She fell asleep armed-in against my chest as we watched *Who's Afraid of Virginia Woolf?*. I never understood how Jackie could doze off in films that bantered so skillfully, but she had always been more of an action film fan, dragging me to every new car chase, shoot-out, bank heist flick that hit the theaters each summer. I sat and watched Elizabeth Taylor quip her seduction across the dance floor of a diner, snide her way through a verbal game she and Richard Burton engaged in for lack of other excitement. I felt oddly summed up, represented in a film made years before my birth. I was afraid of Virginia Woolf, too.

Jackie stirred in time to grab tissues. I watched the credits, unaware of the tears slicking my cheeks. She grabbed my hand and pulled me to the bed, curled beside me. Under blankets we slept unclothed, Jackie's fuzzy arms wrapped around me, her dreams whimpering out, scattered through the night.

We never talked about anything serious and joked our way through the days, caught up in parks and coffee shops. Jackie stayed at my apartment a few nights a week, wrote a new quote for me on the blackboard each visit. She insisted that they last only as long as we were apart and erased the previous quote before scrawling the new one. But every morning when she left, I wrote the words down in a small notebook buried in my pantry behind spices I never touched. I resisted the urge to define us.

We were small town Midwest-awed again, driving up the coast to see the Pacific, hiking through the redwoods, feeling fresh to the views as first time. Revisited tourist spots, drove over CA-299 W in daylight to see the cliffs we'd wound around in foggy dark. Occasionally I convinced Jackie to try a bite of a new cheese, an especially fine truffle I'd bought at the chocolate store, a sip of a whole-fat latte. She suffered the intrusions with a sly smile, as if in on a secret way to sustain her body that I wasn't yet elevated enough to understand, a devoutness to subsisting on air.

III

JACKIE COLLAPSED ON A WEDNESDAY MORNING. Hit her head on a table and collarboned the floor before her roommate discovered her fetal-curled, momentarily awake enough after the fall to close into herself. Even when we sleep, we subconsciously comma our hands, bend the wrists in. The ambulance reached the hospital in minutes and Jackie was blanketed into a 45-degree angled adjustable bed.

She was unconscious when I slipped into the room, didn't notice me steal a butterscotch from the cheap crystal dish on the rolling side table. Her limbs jagged up through the layers of blankets, her wrist-banded arms like toothpicks inside napkin holders set out on her lap. I never understood the description of skin as ashen, but Jackie's was, now, and looked like it would flake off and fly into the corridor with the slightest wind from an opened door or a blown kiss. The monitor beeped out her heart and medicine IVed into her. The tube running up her nostrils and down her throat fed her and I imagined her waking up and clawing at the artificial veins, trying to bite through the food jugular first.

The doctor asked if Jackie had family, who to contact. *Just me*, I said. He explained her to me, the brain muddled that would stay incomplete, her body that rejected the liquid food. The heart stopped for four minutes twice already, too much muscle lost. She weighed seventy pounds. An even-cut number, count in fives when you are little, learning, jump half steps up decades and bases. *You will need to decide to end life support.*

At night I apostrophed myself next to Jackie, arms closed tight against my body. I feared even an arm across her chest would snap her. The machines clicking, toctic sluggish heart beating, compression and drip in plastic bagged medicine every hour marked my night in doses. I slated my thighs between the knob of her hip and metal railing. The two of us weighing little more than an average person, the bed barely creaked, even as I shifted. Jackie never moved.

I ebbed through dreams and visions, waking to every twitched elbow or shoulder, toppling an arm or foot over the side of the bed. The nurses shifted me like an extra limb when they needed to check an IV or change Jackie's colostomy bag. No one tried to send me home, but harbored me into the room instead. They fed me oatmeal in bed, apples waxed too long and mealy, ground Miracle Whipped chicken salad on generic brand square white bread. I toasted Jackie's improved heartbeat with a ginger ale mimosa and caught her up on celebrity gossip from the library of tabloids the nurses carted in. I pretended she heard me.

As she rehydrated, Jackie regained color but not weight. Her atrophied limbs thinned further and she disintegrated before me daily. I called out of work indefinitely, citing a family emergency. When I asked Luke to suitcase some clothes for me he left the bag with the nurses, head turned away from the room. The evening nurse worked primarily in the wing for children with terminal illness and I was the one patient of hers who would live. She spent a half hour with me each night, combing my hair and singing toddler songs. Jackie's hair was too thin to brush, releasing itself in strands without a touch, tufts jumping down from scalp to chin to slight-bend waist. I collected the strands in my fist, ponytailed them in my hand, shoved them in pockets. When I was a child, my mother laminated a lock of my hair to book-mark her diary, another one for her bible. I wanted to lami-nate Jackie, run her through plastic impervious to the world, preserve her for years. My paper doll, I'd set her against the wall and draw her a new dress each day, tape it to the out-lines sealed in plastic. Fake women are allowed to be thin and she'd no longer need food, no one would comment on twig limbs and hollowed cheeks.

Four days. No visitors, me fluttering Jackie's eyelids with tissue hoping for even a reflex blink, doctors ordering new drips, nurses begging too much food into me as if it would transmit to an unconscious body through proximity. Bruises on Jackie's forehead purpling, yellowing, the bump sinking back into her scalp, but her heart still leap-frogging itself, jumping when it should stop and crouch. Brain scanned dead.

Films glamorize a plug pulled, a grieving family watching a remaining ounce of person shudder out when the heart stops beating. When the doctors cut the life support I stayed curled.

She never flickered, no presence rushed through the air, no release sighed through her body. One moment her chest rose, one moment it fell. I slept in her hospital bed as they processed paperwork, woke pillowcased with tear remnants, creaked my cramped limbs to sitting. She had basic insurance through work; did I know her final wishes? *Cremation*, I said.

I HELD JACKIE IN A JAR ABOVE THE PACIFIC OCEAN. At the edge of the continent I watched the sea overtake a small island, minute by minute. Each crash of wave against rock shot seagulls to the air to circle and try again, higher up. My arms ached but I remained outstretched, stood witness to the tide in her place. No one else appeared. Even the surfers who braved the cove when the temperatures dropped to forty never showed as spots below. When the first waves assaulted the island's peak, I unclasped my fingers. The jar dropped to the rocks that phantomed in and out below, sharding the water with glass and powder. Jackie disappeared.

J ACKIE'S ROOMMATE, KELSEY, found a replacement tenant right away and the responsibility of cleaning out Jackie's belongings fell to me. I felt intrusive walking into the bedroom and hushed my way through her closets and drawers. Clothes boxed for donation to a thrift store, I imagined catching a familiar outfit floating around a corner in Arcata, fooling myself into believing it was Jackie, only to discover a young girl had compiled a wardrobe on the cheap. Seeing Jackie in ghosts around town scared me; living with her shadows shifting around an area inextricably linked to our togetherness, too much of a reminder. Some of her books I kept, some I packed with the clothes. Kelsey held onto the furniture for the next renter but when she offered to pay, I refused the cash. The bed and dresser weren't mine to sell. All of the furniture that reminded me of Jackie was arranged across my studio.

When I found Jackie's stash of diaries dating back to elementary school, I impulsed first to read, then throw out, then hold onto for future reference. I felt uncomfortable about invading, but equally so about not knowing what was really going on in Jackie's house and family, her mind as she starved to death, her perceptions of me. So I slipped the journals into my letter carrier shoulder bag and gave myself seventy-two hours to work up the courage to read them or throw them in the trash when it went out on Thursday morning.

I vacuumed Jackie's room, washed the windows, made the bed with fresh sheets I'd found in the closet just in case the new roommate had forgotten to purchase or pack some. Washed the dishes still left in the kitchen sink that I knew could not have belonged to Jackie. Cleaned the bathroom. Mopped the kitchen floor. The last of my nervous and grieving energy exhausted, I left the key on the counter and let myself out, final-relinquishing Jackie's space for both of us.

AT HOME, THE DIARIES STARED AT ME for three days while I alternated between red wine, white wine, joints, and espresso chip ice cream. Bruce brought me curry from Japhy's, ham and cheese croissants from the café, premade salads from Wildberries, a new meal every day for a week. He gave me a gift certificate for a massage. Passed me the business card of an alternative medicine counselor-cum-homeopathic healer. Luke came with him one evening to reminisce half-heartedly with us about Jackie and to tell me he would be moving back east at the end of the month. He let me hug him goodbye, kissed my forehead, but wouldn't discuss his plans further.

I ran down the stairs in the early morning when I heard the rumble of the dumptruck cresting the hill by my studio and tossed the paper bag of diaries into the trashcan just as the driver curbsided. *Just made it!* smiled the guy as he jumped from the small platform at the back where he handheld himself to the truck, up and down the streets of Arcata. *Lucky me.*

EVERY FRIDAY AFTERNOON the women lined up along one edge of the Plaza dressed head-to-toe in black, hands empty, mouths closed and never speaking. They stood for two hours, stared at the traffic, at the pedestrians, at nothing. Watched the world around them pass without interacting with it or each other. Some days there was a whole crowd of them, some days only one or two. They stood in the rain as it washed over their faces, soaked through their coats and up into their shoes.

When I tried to talk to one of the women, she continued staring straight in front of her, a pursed-lip non-frown plastered beneath uncommitted eyebrows that gave away how much she had to work to keep from answering my questions. I wanted to know who they were, why they were there, what would make you stand in the rain for hours without speaking. Some of the women seemed to know each other, acknowledging presence with a slight nod when they convened, but I wasn't certain if this camaraderie was from outside of the assembly or from weeks of silent street standing together.

I asked my boss at the record store about the women.

"They're protesting war," he said. "Violence. Human rights abuses. It's not just in Arcata, it's an international protest. Women just show up for it and disperse afterward."

I craved protest, an outside release of anxiety and aimlessness foundationed in a cause, something to believe in strongly enough that it would consume my anger and blot out the exhaustion taking over my body from waking up night after night wondering where Jackie was. The following Friday, the absence of color covered my arms, chest, stomach, legs, and I walked to the corner of the Plaza where one of the women I'd asked repeatedly for an explanation hinted a smile my way and went back to staring. I sectioned off a small space for myself, stood still, wondering at the appropriate expression. Should I appear sullen, calm, at the peace for which I was protesting, friendly, standoffish? There should be rules, must be rules, why didn't I look them up before I got involved?

An hour passes slowly when all it presents is thoughts mixed with self-conscious performance unease. Far from feeling as though I were making a difference, I felt I was wasting time; I had chosen an un-organization at random, a cause for which I cared but wasn't passionate, simply to ease my own pain, not the suffering of others. I watched a spider crawl over my foot, hesitate, turn and climb back over and set off toward his origination. A car honked and Dustin waved, yelled joking catcalls. A young girl in jeans I'd seen for sale at a local boutique for $175 and designer sunglasses propped herself crosslegged near my feet and set out a cup and small cardboard sign.

I protested in black for three weeks, waiting for the satisfaction to hit me, for the calming feeling I imagined arrived when you made a difference. But each Friday I found myself further distracted, my protest meaning less and less as my thoughts drifted to every topic but war. Had someone approached me to ask what I was doing, as I had approached the other protestors a month before, I would have shook my head, shrugged, and slumped up the street to change into colorful clothes. But no one asked, so I planted myself until I could no longer justify it.

Luke sent me a card from Boston, enveloped with another letter from his parents. He was doing well, had returned to college to finish up his degree, felt less ambiguous on the east coast. While still not certain where he would go next, he knew he would get there. Had he stayed in Arcata, he wrote, he never would have left, you know? I did. He encouraged me to leave, if only for a trip, to free my mind from the complacency of the town and the memories of Jackie. Told me I could crash at his place for a night if I ever made it to Boston. Said he'd like me to meet his new girlfriend, thought I would like her. *She's right for me*, he wrote.

His parents had heard of Jackie's death, of Luke's and my dissolution, of the lost baby. When Luke told them, he must have left out the more privately painful parts: my infidelity, our arguing, my hospitalization. They seemed to consider me an honorary daughter. Perhaps Bruce, who had remained im-

164

partial throughout our west coast tenure, had been the one to update them, run middle ground reporter.

Was I planning on applying to any of those colleges they'd sent me information on? Were there any other schools of interest? What were my plans for the coming months? If I would like to join them for a couple weeks at their summer home in August, please let them know, they'd love to see me. I was stunned and confused by their openness to me.

When I sat to write to both Luke and his parents, I realized I had no plan, no sense of the next year. What could I say in my letters except that I continued to work at the record shop and trim weed? I had a cheap studio and a pile of cash in Bruce's safe that grew weekly but never seemed enough to decide to move on.

Entwined in Jackie's self-disassembly, I'd been oblivious to my succumbing to the stagnancy of the region, to the motionless pattern of my life, the slow dissolution of resolve as I waited for something to happen. We'd relegated our adventurous selves to the two girls who crossed the country in a semi-stolen car and busked their way to Cali. I'd so defined myself by crossing the country and breaking childhood imprinted taboos that I'd forgotten to continue the evolution once we'd settled into Arcata. My identity was fused with Jackie's, with the worry of her bony frame and the outlines her fingers drew across my fear. Now that she was gone, I was paralyzed in an unsettled complacency, knowing I needed movement but unable to decide on a motion.

I pulled out the folder where I had filed the college brochures, looked up the schools online, ran a search for others, and made a list divided by location. West coast or east coast. I couldn't imagine returning to the Midwest. I applied for the following year's spring semester at a handful of schools, coaxing confidence into my fingertips each time I clicked "send."

I fell asleep imagining a campus, trees, dorms like the ones I'd seen in brochure photographs, preppy kids smiling at nerdy kids smiling at goth kids, all one happy integrated scholastic family. Jackie walked to me across the college quad, the large grassy expanse shrinking as she broke into a run toward me, weight reappearing on her arms, legs, stomach with each gallop. We hooked arms and left campus for our apartment to study homework, each other, our new city. Reinvented.

IN AUGUST, I PRETENDED MYSELF PART OF LUKE'S FAMILY, spent two weeks at his parents' lake house as a long-lost daughter returned. We played Scrabble and drank after-dinner cocktails on the porch, laughed our way through an old family photo album. Luke's father seemed more relaxed in their vacation spot, but I stayed careful not to contradict him. His mother and I mostly listened to his diatribes and smiled occasionally at each other, content to be quiet and keep the peace.

We built a campfire each night, drove up the coast to their favorite beach. The Atlantic barely resembled the Pacific, except in its endless stretching away from me. I learned to pronounce words with the New England rich a—baanaaaana and caaaan't—and how to eat a lobster.

Luke arrived in time to float across the lake with me for an afternoon. We took the first hour to settle out of awkwardness, paddling aimlessly from dock to raft and back. Loaded into their pedal boat, we footed our way in silence toward a series of rocks jetting out of the water at the far end of the lake.

"The loons have nested here every year since I was a little kid," said Luke. "My dad used to take us out so we could see the mothers swim away from the rocks with the newborns riding on their backs across the water. When I was seven, Bruce and his friends took out our canoes late at night, told me they were going to look at the babies sleeping. I was so excited, felt so grown up, when they asked me to come along. But when we got there, the guys grabbed a chick and threw him into the water, just chucked him in, laughing, saying they would teach him to swim. Like human toddlers. I dove out of the canoe, but couldn't get to the baby in time. The mother wailed and dove again and again. Everyone laughed, except Bruce. He told the guys to go to hell and jumped in. We swam back together in the dark."

We stared at the rocks, slowing our feet as we approached, letting ourselves coast. We watched as two loons approached, the chick already swimming on his own, darting across the lake with his mother. Luke told me loons mate for life and I felt odd thinking of them as birds. They bansheed away from us, announcing themselves to the camps dotting around the cove bend, mourning the approaching end of summer.

"So, how's the new girlfriend?" I asked and we both laughed, released the tension to shudder into the lake, down below the small waves slapping the edge of the boat.

"Amy? She's great. I don't think you two would ever be close friends, but I think you'd like her. She keeps me driven and is crazy about me almost to the point of being obnoxious. But, she knows what she wants." Luke hooked his arm around my shoulders and kissed above my right ear. "You and I never did."

"Yeah. Maybe it was Arcata."

"Maybe."

We stared across the water.

"I'm starting college in February," I said. "Going to head up to Oregon."

"You'll love it, getting involved and interested, feeling like you're moving toward something."

"Yeah. I'm not ready to leave the west coast, but I can't stay in northern Cali anymore. Everywhere I go is a shadow of us, of Jackie, of something I never defined."

He left his arm around me and we drifted. A boat cranked by, towing a skier, and we rocked sideways into and out of the wake. We stayed for hours, slowed, taking turns jumping in, climbing out of the water, ignoring the sun crackling our shoulders to red.

"I'm driving back across country alone," I told Luke. "Going to buy a cheap car and work myself through the same spaces we traveled two years ago. I might even try to sleep in the same rest stops."

Luke half-expressed his face, unsure of whether to concern or congratulate. I imagined him shuffling through polite ways to say he worried about the trip triggering too many memories, sending me into a grieving paralysis.

"I need to redefine the places as mine," I whispered. "Make sure this country and I exist outside of Jackie-imprinted photographs."

LUKE HUGGED ME GOODBYE and asked me to come to Boston for a visit, but I wasn't ready to see him contextualized into a new life, a new woman. We promised to write and call. His parents sold me an old car they'd been keeping at the camp for jostling into town; they tried to give it to me, insisting it was worth only junk prices, but I was uncomfortable accepting the gift. They'd already arranged for a partial scholarship through my college, pressuring someone in the administration who owed them a favor. I picked wildflowers for Luke's mother and cried when I left them.

THE EASTERN STATES BLURRED PAST my windows. I crossed through New York, Pennsylvania, Ohio, Indiana as quickly as possible, wanting to over-with my upcoming stop in Illinois. When I telephoned my mother to tell her I would be driving across the country and would like to grab dinner and meet Mark, I suggested we convene in Chicago, one of their favorite cities and a neutral ground to me. She hesitated, catching her voice on anger or tears I couldn't distinguish, but ultimately agreed that dinner in town would be fine. Anything but fine seemed more accurate to me, but I guilted myself into seeing her before I resolidified to the west coast, enrolled to the region for another four years.

I parked in a suburb and took the train into Chicago. With hours before dinner, I wandered the city, awed at the massive Picasso and Calder sculptures downtown, sat by the lions at the entrance to the museum. The city seemed bent on its food so I ate a boiled hot dog slathered in mustard, ketchup, relish, chopped onions; downed a slice of deep dish pizza that made any substitute seem shallow in description and size. I took the

El, feeling, from years of films, that this was quintessential Chicago. The hour before dinner I spent sitting at Navy Pier, looking out over Lake Michigan. The water stretched so far from me that it disappeared like the ocean and seagulls circled above. Even though there were no tides or surf I couldn't reconcile the water to my idea of lake, the expanse covering too much silt not to bleed into other waters and connect other lands in my mind. I imagined Jackie's ashes washing up at my feet, miles of tidal swells and rocking bringing her back to me, over invisible oceans, into the giant lake so close to where we began.

I WALKED INTO THE RESTAURANT to discover Mark was taller than I expected and I wondered at forgetting my mother's height, how she rises within an inch of me. I awkwardly hugged my mother and she squeezed back, aching her months of pain into me, cutting off my breath. I was tempted to apologize, didn't, but my mother saw the creases in my face she knew from years watching me sorry my way through our tension and she nodded slightly. We were seated immediately.

I asked benign questions, daughterly questions: *How is work going, Mark? Do you like your new house? How was the honeymoon? Do you ever visit the farmhouse?* I received cordial answers, snippets of polite mixed with if-you'd-been-involved-you'd-already-know. They asked me nothing through the appetizers.

"So, I'm starting college in the spring," I reported.

"Oh, that is lovely, I'd always hoped you'd get a degree," my mother said.

"What will you be studying?" asked Mark.

"I think photography."

"Shouldn't you consider something more practical, honey?"

"Let her find herself," Mark sideways mumbled. "You'll choose another major to complement it, of course. No one makes a living as a photographer, and you strike me as a very practical young lady."

I stared at Mark, ran my knife in short slices across the porcelain salad plate. He grew uncomfortable, looked around for the waiter, to my mother, imploring anyone to save him from me.

"Actually, I'm an aspiring starving artist."

My mother tried to change the subject.

"I'm sorry you had to deal with Jackie's father, dear, that must have been upsetting. How is she taking it?"

I could see her wondering at my silence, at the forced composure that worked its way down through my face, my gritted teeth clamping down to close back the tears. Mark seemed relieved by the shift in my mood off of him and onto my mother.

"Jackie's dead."

We stared at the entrees the food runners placed in front of us. Mark ordered another glass of scotch and a bottle of wine for the table. My mother's cheeks slicked with tears but she must have been wearing waterproof mascara.

"I'm sorry, honey," she choked out. "I know she was a close friend."

"You are so fucking naïve."

"Excuse me? I know you must be hurting but that is no way for a lady to speak, needless to mention we are out at dinner!" My mother hissed, Mark wondering whether to jump in or stay out.

"Jackie and I were in love." I watched her forehead puzzle, a swallow repeat itself in her throat but move nowhere.

"You mean you loved each other. Of course you did, sweetheart."

"No. I mean what I said, we were in love. I mean we dated. I mean we fucked each other."

She grabbed Mark's arm, nails digging, breathed sharply in sighs I remembered so well from childhood but had almost forgotten in the years away. I wondered at how we rewrite each other, smudge out the sharp to blur, file down the razor edges that cut us into straight lines of mother and daughter. At how easily the lines are redrawn, crisp and critical again. I pushed away from the table and walked out of the restaurant, my mother's tears flowing enough to run her mascara and eyeliner now, her sorrow at my revelation, not Jackie's death.

She called me once, six months into college, to apologize for dinner going so wrong, to wish she had handled my news differently, to tell me there are people I can talk to about my misguided attraction. To ask if I will let her pray for me. I told her to pray for whatever she wants because her God forgot to allow for people.

We will never speak again, never dinner together. Our existence to each other will be relegated to occasional Christmas and Birthday cards, and she will join my father in a double-frame I store in a bedside table, on a closet shelf, in a box below the bed.

THE DAYS STARTED LATER, ended earlier, than they had when Jackie and I left at the beginning of summer more than two years before. The earth felt older as my tires dusted through Iowa. I skirted around our farmhouse, circled through the town, debating back and forth whether to drive past and look from the car. I wanted to fix the memories I'd somehow formed so incompletely, wanted to account for an entirely different childhood than I realized I'd lived. I drove away without stopping, needing to preserve something. The memory of my small town growing up seemed like the easiest thing to leave intact.

I couldn't remember the rest stops where we'd spent our first nights, the details of which generic parking lot with toilets a step up from outhouse and vending machines filled with coffee, soda, and gummy candies had cradled our car in lights while Jackie shivered. The roads looked familiar in the discomforting way of did I see this from here or television or falsified memory. I stopped by the Welcome to Nebraska sign and self-portraited. The photograph felt empty.

As I stretched out of Nebraska, I shook my head at the several-stories-high white Jesus monument, arms spread wide, overlooking the edge of the city where it met the sparse landscape. Plaster or painted metal, his eyes looked empty, all the same bright white run into his face, into his long hair, into his robes. I imagined it must be lonely, being the son of a god who forced you into loving the people who used your name for fighting. Even if someone believed you were divine, you'd have to remind them that others claimed that for you. Those weren't your words. I watched Jesus shrink in my rearview mirror, immobile and silent.

Wyoming, same pink. I worked my way through gas stations, across the highway, windows down with music loud enough to announce me to the next meter of road. The country spread out slower this time, and I lounged in it, unhurried. I made my way through dinners and random conversations, choosing every stop and detour and sidetrip on my own. I'd never known this independence, even with Jackie. I'd never been emotionally self-sufficient.

In Nevada, I found the megaplex where we'd joined with Luke's group. At least, the massive gas station appeared to be the same one. I imagined the car still sitting, abandoned, but it was gone, towed or stolen away years before. Still too young to purchase beer, I considered mimicking Jackie and finding a willing guy. I drove out of the lot without even climbing out of the car, toward the customs booths and California.

I wanted to feel different, wanted to see each sunrise
with colors more vibrant or muted, any change to distinguish
between before and now. But the only difference I felt was
distance from a trip that had solidified in my mind as story,
great adventure, a pilgrimage away from cornfields to independence. Trekking over the same roads both completed and
distanced the story. When I hit the winding curves of northern California, I was shocked with realization. The trip felt
complete without Jackie.

When I reached my studio and settled to the bedspread, I
was happily exhausted, my arms and legs elevated in celebration of a 3,000 mile journey alone. In a few months, I could
begin packing for Oregon, for a dorm shared with a random
roommate, for a life fully on my own. I fell asleep, dreaming
snapshots of Jackie in desert and Jackie absent, an unknown
girl with her arm linked in mine, mist and rain and clouds
that rolled orange overhead. Danny fading to blend with
Jackie, arching over Wyoming as I sunset my way back home.

B RUCE THREW ME A GOODBYE PARTY, even though I
heard about it beforehand and begged him not to. The
event felt like a summation of my time in Arcata, the
growers, the trimmers, the few friends I'd made outside of that
circle and in the record shop. Dustin and Nick put together a
slideshow of photographs from the past couple of years, moments I'd forgotten or ignored or not known were recorded.
Luke and Jackie appeared on the wall, sections of them blotted
out when someone walked in front of the projector or raised
a glass to toast too high. We drank and smoked and repeated
ourselves, *just like old times* somebody said and was right. For
all that was different, so little had changed.

BEFORE I LEFT ARCATA FOR THE FINAL TIME I bought another
box of Crane stationary and wrote Jackie a long letter. Of
things she knew: the fog that ends in a straight line across the
highway when you approach Blue Lake, the smell of herb lingering in the washing machines at the laundromat, the Plaza
filled with students and performance artists and girls in brand

new jeans and boots panhandling. Of the damp mulch lining the pathway through the redwood grove in town, the picnic benches where we'd sat with guitars and played to the trunks of trees. Of the Pacific crashing against the cliffs in Trinidad.

I wanted to write to her about Danny, about the twin I held first. How when he ran his fingers across my arms I felt closer to her. Of the blankets we brought to cornfields to watch the fireflies while we kissed and slid hands below hips, across ribs, over backs and legs. Of the parsley and a decision I made when we were only beginning to realize we would understand the opposite of our parents' beliefs. That we could walk away. I longed to explain how I spent the past years feeling I was to blame for Danny, that he told me months before the rope that he couldn't live with what we'd done. How I believed he'd shake it, realize we were no more wrong than we'd been for spending nights outside in the tree fort, recognize we were allowed to disagree. Of not noticing the undertone of *Yeah, I'm fine* weeks later.

Instead, I filled pages with the story of crossing from one life into another. Retold ourselves in ink so we'd never stop repeating memories, so we'd last as long as the outlines of our photographs. I sorted through albums, writing each color in location, Wyoming pink, Nevada orange, California green and blue; telling each posed smile as part of ourselves. When I placed the letter into the ocean, the water spread the ink until the translucent sheets floated grey and tossed back and forth through the foam on the shore. I gathered and balled them, threw the weight as far into the sea as I could. Whispered *Sorry.*

WHEN I DIE, my body will join Danny in the earth, Jackie in the sea. The last traces of me will dissolve back into the soil. If my life ends before my mother's, she will mourn the loss of a child not once, but as an eternal sacrifice. She will be drawn by a revisionist's desire to change the story of my existence post-passing, rewrite me as pious, even if misdirected. Perhaps my mother will convince herself God called me home early, an Icarus straying too close to unforgiven. With her surmising and retelling, she will save her own spirit, not mine. My soul will rest the moment my brain stops sending signals.

Sometimes the hospital closes in on me, waiting patiently, just out of reach and just in sight. Its blurry boundary threatens to overtake me, pull me back. Threatens to whisper to lovers, to me, that I have fallen apart before and could again. That I know unstable. I watch the shadow warily, aware that I have replaced an old fear with a new one.

AT NIGHT I DREAM OF DYING, of my hand in Jackie's, of an isolated trail in the Redwood National Park. We find the tallest tree and dig our nails into the side, climb the ancient bark without leaving fingerprints, sit on the highest limb supported by a cloud of needles. We inhale the damp mixed with airborne soil and light a final joint. I still cough when I try to hold the smoke in my lungs but I no longer grow drowsy. She asks me if I remember running my hands down her concave stomach and I reach for her. We climb higher, tiptoe in flip-flops on leaves as we grab onto the fog and pull ourselves into the air. Jackie kisses me and I relearn her pressure, the way her mouth pushes and folds, the space when her lips gap. We dangle from droplets suspended in the sky, hovering between exalted and fallen.

Acknowledgements

For courage and love, thank you Dominic Miller. You are my greatest joy. For mentoring, showing me how to write, and holding me to high standards, thank you Ryan Boudinot. For insight and encouragement, thank you Jocelyn Cullity. For kind words, poetic perspective, and an eye for detail, thank you Walter Butts. You are sorely missed. For dear friendship and endless reading recommendations, thank you Josh Amses. For challenging and expanding my views, and the many years of fun, thank you Drew Lundgren, Ed Atkinson, Meg Dunfee, Amber McZeal, Ron Heacock, Corey Gleisberg, Jonathan Smucker, Melissa Parker, Jason Stocks, Lane Watson, Ryan Brown, and Clay River. Forever, for your friendship and wisdom, thank you Adam Ruhf.

Fomite

A fomite is a medium capable of transmitting infectious organisms from one individual to another.

"The activity of art is based on the capacity of people to be infected by the feelings of others." Tolstoy, *What Is Art?*

Writing a review on Amazon, Good Reads, Shelfari, Library Thing or other social media sites for readers will help the progress of independent publishing. To submit a review, go to the book page on any of the sites and follow the links for reviews. Books from independent presses rely on reader to reader communications.

Visit http://www.fomitepress.com/FOMITE/Our_Books.html for more information or to order any of our books.

As It Is On Earth
Peter M Wheelwright

Dons of Time
Greg Guma

Loisaida
Dan Chodorkoff

My Father's Keeper
Andrew Potok

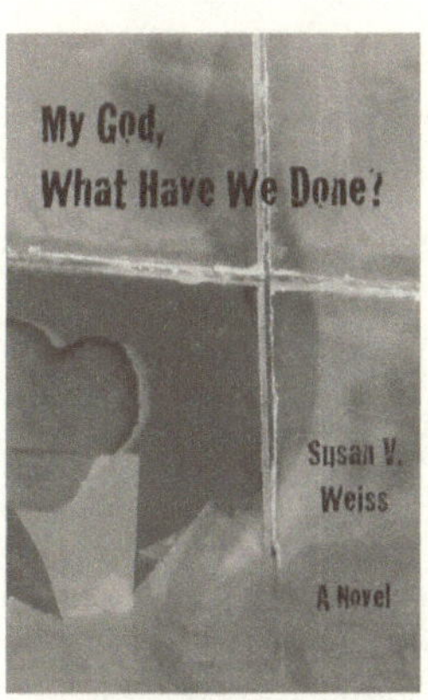

My God, What Have We Done
Susan V Weiss

Rafi's World
Fred Russell

Fomite

The Co-Conspirator's Tale
Ron Jacobs

Short Order Frame Up
Ron Jacobs

All the Sinners Saints
Ron Jacobs

Travers' Inferno
L. E. Smith

The Consequence of Gesture
L. E. Smith

Raven or Crow
Joshua Amses

Sinfonia Bulgarica
Zdravka Evtimova

The Good Muslim
of Jackson Heights
Jaysinh Birjépatil

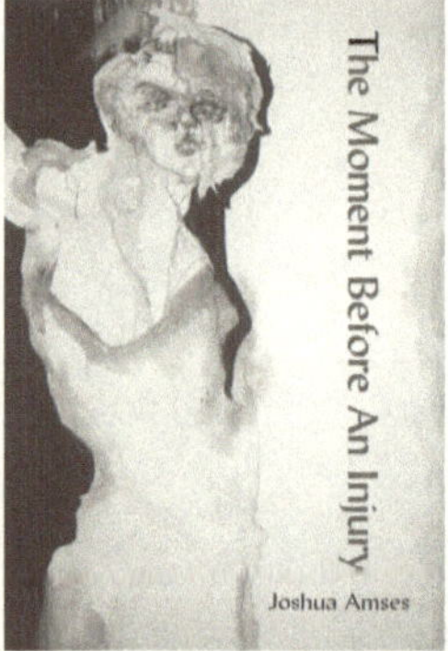

The Moment Before an Injury
Joshua Amses

The Return of
Jason Green
Suzi Wizowaty

Victor Rand
David Brizeri

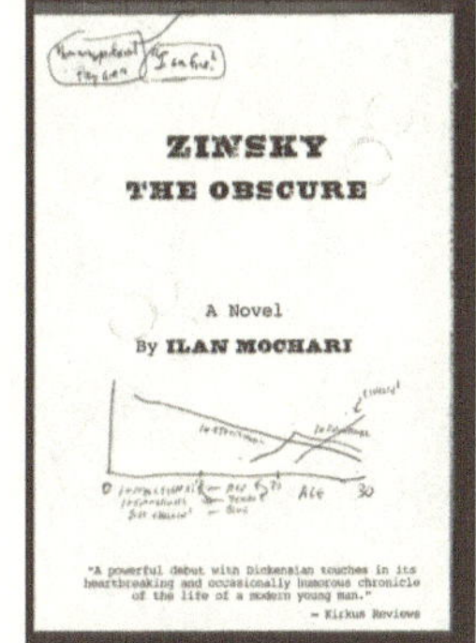

Zinsky the Obscure
Ilan Mochari

Body of Work
Andrei Guruianu

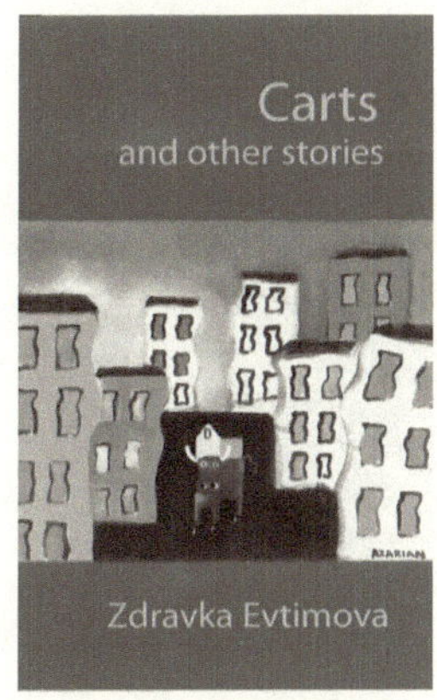

Carts and Other Stories
Zdravka Evtimova

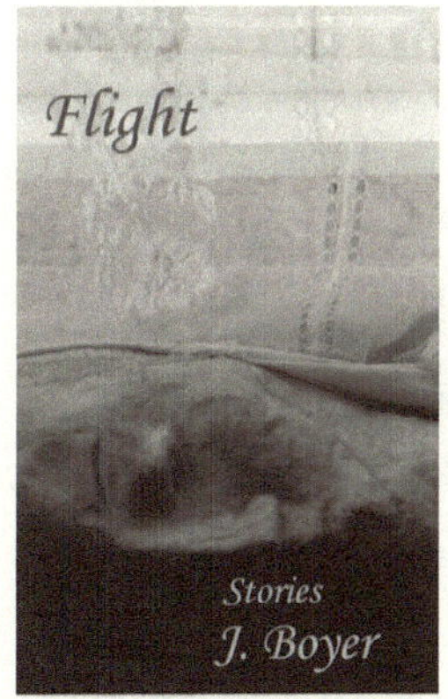

Flight
Jay Boyer

Love's Labours
Jack Pulaski

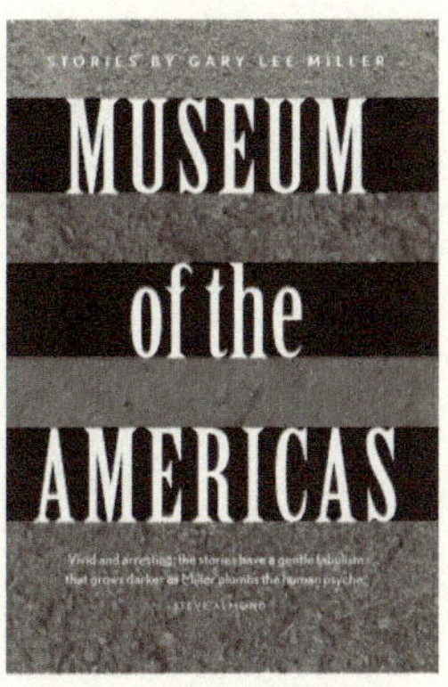

Museum of the Americas
Gary Lee Miller

Saturday Night at Magellan's
Charles Rafferty

Fomite

Signed Confessions
Tom Walker

Still Time
Michael Cocchiarale

Suite for Three Voices
Derek Furr

Unfinished Stories of Girls
Catherine Zobal Dent

Views Cost Extra
L. E. Smith

Visiting Hours
Jennifer Anne Moses

When You Remeber
Deir Yassin
R. L. Green

Alfabestiaro
Antonello Borra

Cycling in Plato's Cave
David Cavanagh

AlphaBetaBestiario
Antonello Borra

Entanglements
Tony Magistrale

Everyone Lives Here
Sharon Webster

Four-Way Stop
Sherry Olson

Improvisational
Arguments
Anna Faktorovitch

Loosestrife
Greg Delanty

Meanwell
Janice Miller Potter

Roadworthy Creature
Roadworth Craft
Kate Magill

The Derivation of
Cowboys & Indians
Joseph D. Reich

The Housing Market
Joseph D. Reich

The Empty Notebook
Interrogates Itself
Susan Thomas

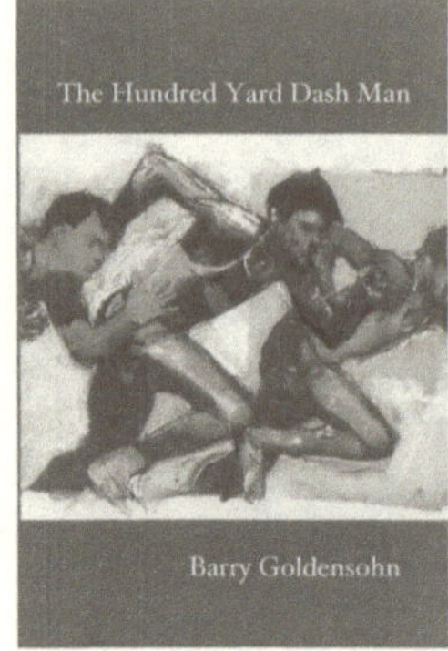

The Hundred Yard
Dash Man
Barry Goldensohn

The Listener Aspires
to the Condition of Music
Barry Goldensohn

The Way None
of This Happened
Mike Breiner

Screwed
Stephen Goldberg

Planet Kasper
Peter Schumann

My Murder
and Other Local News
David Schein

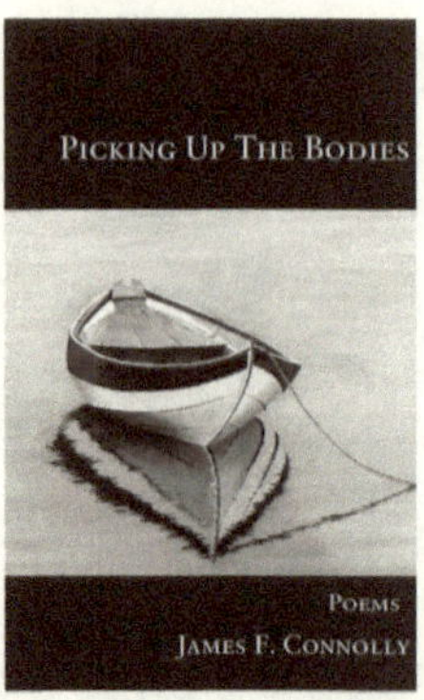

Picking Up the Bodies
James F. Connolly

Fomite

The Falkland Quartet
Tony Whedon

Among Angelic Orders
Susan Thomas